D0014746

THE LUNATIC AT LARGE

BY
J. STORER CLOUSTON

INTRODUCTION BY
JONATHAN AMES

THE COLLINS LIBRARY
[A DIV. OF McSWEENEY'S BOOKS]

McSWEENEY'S BOOKS
SAN FRANCISCO

www.mcsweeneys.net

The Collins Library is a series of newly edited and
typeset editions of unusual out-of-print books.

Editor: Paul Collins
Assistant Editor: Jennifer Elder

With special thanks to Glen David Gold,
without whom this title would not have been rediscovered.

The photograph on the previous page shows Leon Errol
in the title role of the 1927 silent movie adaptation of *The Lunatic at Large*.
Still photo reproduced from *Mid-Week Pictorial* of February 10, 1927.
No copy of the film is known to exist.

The Lunatic at Large was first published in 1899 by William Blackwood & Sons, London.

ISBN: 1-932416-70-6

ABOUT THIS BOOK

Some books can only be discovered in picturesque settings: propping up a creaky table in a seaside cottage, say, or hidden under a sleeping cat in a used bookstore. Such books claim no great importance or attention for themselves, but live on through singular acts of charmed discovery, passed along in battered vintage copies from one friend and one decade to the next.

The Lunatic at Large is just such a book. The tale of the newest resident of Clankwood, home of "the best-bred lunatics in England," its release in 1899 introduced an unsuspecting Victorian public to one Mr. Francis Beveridge.... At least, Beveridge *seems* to be his name, as it's the one sewn into all his clothes. But rather than attending his asylum's Saturday dances, Beveridge prefers to attempt escapes, leaving his asylum attendants in red-faced pursuit. So when the traveling German noble Baron Rudolf von Blitzenberg finds himself at the luxurious Hôtel Mayonaise without a guide to this strange land's customs, who better to help him than the curiously amnesiac Englishman who materializes by his side?

The Lunatic at Large passed the sparkling chalice of comic banter from Oscar Wilde to P.G. Wodehouse; its bestselling success came just four years after Wilde's final play *The Importance of Being Earnest*, and three years before Wodehouse's first novel *The Pothunters*. The three writers might be said to walk arm in arm, rather like the Baron and the Lunatic vacationing at the seaside. Clouston proved nearly as prolific as Wodehouse in the half-century that followed, with books ranging from a murderous comedy of errors (*His First Offense,* 1912) to thrillers (*The Spy in Black,* 1917) and the visionary 1933 robot farce *Button Brains.* But to his public, Clouston forever remained the author of *The Lunatic at Large.* It stands alone in Victorian literature as a story that goes over the top and stays there, mockingly refusing to climb back down. It's unapologetically and amorally funny, with a trickster hero who perpetrates merry outrages simply for the hell of it. And he has a perfect foil in the Baron Rudolph von Blitzenberg—a straight-man who remains as intelligent and sympathetic as his anarchic companion.

Joseph Storer Clouston was nearly the antithesis of his reckless comic creation. Born in 1870 to one of the most ancient families of the Orkney Islands, Clouston attended Oxford and passed the bar in 1895; he went on to serve as Scotland's agricultural subcomissioner, chair of the Orkney Harbours Commissioners, and was one of Orkney's longest-serving Conveners, effectively serving as the head of the local government from his family homestead of Smoogro House. While his Lunatic was a man without a family history, Clouston could trace his own Orkney lineage directly back to the twelfth century and the invading Viking clan of Klo. He remains one of the preeminent chroniclers of Orkney history, and indeed continued to write local antiquarian histories right up until his death in 1944.

But inevitably, what his public clamored for was more lunacy. "Bonker," the Baron's hapless mispronunciation of his companion's alias, even entered the English language as the byword for merry lunacy: bonkers. And so there were many Lunatic sequels—all amusing, but none a patch on their unruly ancestor. But inevitably, what his public clamored for was more lunacy. Where Clouston's work truly gained new life was in the magic new medium being launched by the Lumiere brothers just as *The Lunatic at Large* arrived in bookshops. *His First Offence* was transmuted by revered French director Marcel Carné into *Drole de Drame* (1937), a pinnacle of 1930s French cinema. The next year director Michael Powell and screenwriter Emeric Pressburger filmed *The Spy in Black* to produce the hit *U-Boat 29*. But it was *The Lunatic at Large* that first proved irresistible to filmmakers: the book was made into a silent movie on no less than three occasions, in 1910, 1921, and 1927. The last featured the rubbery vaudeville star Leon Errol in the title role, complete with a madcap sequence of him careening around London in a blimp. Today no trace remains of these silent films; we only have the mute testimony of movie stills in yellowing newspapers.

The Lunatic at Large has suffered a nearly equal and inexplicable era of neglect as a book; it last appeared in U.S. bookstores in 1926, though it was specially reissued in World War II in an Armed Services Edition, an ironic reminder of a time when one might still befriend a gregarious German. But then, the Lunatic always did have a knack for showing up unannounced in odd places. If there was ever a novel meant to be affably abandoned at a summer cabin for the next guest, or read at the beach with sand in its pages, this is that book. Do not imprison it in a bookcase. Let it climb the walls of your little Clankwood, and once again run cheerfully amok out in the wide world.

—*Paul Collins*
Iowa City
June 2006

INTRODUCTION

by JONATHAN AMES

About forty-five minutes ago, I was walking on Fourth Avenue in Seattle, on my way to the city's futuristic library, with the intention, now being realized, of trying to write my introduction to *The Lunatic at Large*. And as I walked I began to write, in my head, how I might begin, and this sentence came to mind: "I have never been possessed by the feeling, or, rather, the wish, that I had written a book I had just read, but *The Lunatic at Large* provoked such a desire—I wish I had written it."

Then, as I waited at the library's entrance for it to open, I decided against that sentence. It seemed like something that had been said before and too many times at that. It also seemed self-important and self-centered—who cares what I might wish for, and how dare I ever presume—even as a wish—that I could write something so brilliant? Also, when I had seen other writers—usually in blurbs—express such a sentiment, it always struck me as jealousy, praise turned into something gross and envious, so I had always morally and snobbishly, I guess, dismissed such statements.

So why had I now thought such a thing? And why have I never thought such a thing before, besides moral snobbism?

I think it had never occurred to me before because of my more or less unconscious acknowledgment—now vaguely conscious—that a book is as singular as its author's DNA, thumbprint, dental x-rays, social-security number, and whatever else it is that is unique unto a person; and so that any one book could only be produced by one person. Thus, why bother wishing that I had written, for example, *The Lunatic at Large?* It simply is not possible, I previously had reasoned on an unconscious level. And yet I had this wish, this thought, as I walked on Fourth Avenue in Seattle.

(I happen to be visiting this city for a few days and my hotel room has no desk, and on the other side of the thin wall there is the constant chatter of a small child, who never seems to leave the room, and yet I cannot hear the parent's reply to this chattering. For some reason only the child's voice, somewhat grating, can be heard, and so combining tourism with the dual necessity of escaping my room and writing this introduction, I came to this rather glorious glass and steel, Rem Koolhaas–designed library. And while I'm on this parenthetical tangent, I would like to say that Rem Koolhaas has the perfect name for an architect; he is Dutch and I don't know what Kool means in Dutch or if Haas means house in Dutch, but it certainly sounds like Koolhaas means "Coolhouse" and that is quite ideal, I think, for an architect. Anyway, let me return to the subject at hand—)

So why have this odd wish now? Well, I think it has something to do with the fact that I have not worked on a novel for some time, nearly three years, and I'm in that state of mind, common to novelists, where I am uncertain whether I will ever be able to write a novel again. And I have to say that the only thing that gives me some vague sense of meaning in an ephemeral and confusing life—a life lived on a tormented, mad planet; well, the planet is not mad but the world of man is definitely insane—is the writing of novels. When working on a book, I feel like I'm doing something quasi-worthwhile since the act of creation is essentially positive, and if what I write brings a handful of middle-class people some distraction, laughter, and happiness, well, then I've done *something,* however meager. But not having worked on a book for some time, I'm scared that I will never have meaning again, and so I selfishly wished that I had written *The Lunatic at Large,* or, actually, and more accurately, what I think I wished was that I could somehow steal *The Lunatic at Large,* change a few details, and attach my name to it since the book has been so long out of print. But that's not quite it, either, I don't think, since I've just said that the writing of a book is what gives me meaning, not slapping my name on stolen goods and taking credit for it. You see, I'm not a deep thinker. I'm a muddled thinker. And I've got myself in a muddle. Why did I have to have that thought on Fourth Avenue?

Let me try to extricate myself. What I like to do when I write—not in this tangled intro I'm afraid—is give the reader pleasure, and *The Lunatic at Large* had given me enormous pleasure, and so what I was wishing for, longing for, was the ability to give a reader pleasure, just as *Lunatic* had pleased me. It's not unlike an impotent man wishing he could make love. Gandhi said—I think it was Gandhi—that violence begets violence begets violence. The converse would be love begets love begets love. And a subset of that, of love, would be pleasure begets pleasure begets pleasure. You receive pleasure and then you want to give pleasure. So in this case, *Lunatic* gave me pleasure and it made me want to give pleasure. A daisy chain of pleasure. But because I feel impotent—can't write—I wished I had written *The Lunatic at Large,* since I don't think I can write books anymore. And, therefore, I could at least have the end result of a meaningful process—the reward, the finished product. Something like that. More muddle—dammit! I apologize if I've made a mess of things.

What else can I tell you? When I sat down at this pleasant gray desk here in the library I had a view, in the distance, of Puget Sound. Then, right after I plugged in my laptop, a homeless-appearing man—mid-thirties, beard, tiny face (small nose, chin, and mouth), eyes too close together, long greasy hair, stained vinyl jacket—sat directly across from me, which was mildly upsetting in the same sort of way as when you're sitting on an airplane and at the last moment someone takes the seat next to you.

Actually, it was more than upsetting—it was a bit maddening, because there were a dozen empty desks all around us and yet he sat right in front of me blocking, somewhat, my view of the Sound—a view of the Sound is a pretty good bit of language, if you think about it—and, also, not to be rude, he smells pretty bad. It's a mix of sweat and tobacco and street and unwashed hair. So he has blocked my view and he has violated my overly sensitive nostrils.

I've tolerated this smell because I'm lazy—I had already plugged myself in—and, also, I didn't want him to think that I was put off by proximity to his person. Furthermore, I thought that since I'm writing about *The Lunatic at Large* it would only be fitting that I have a lunatic sitting across from me since he does seem to have a touch of lunacy about him. He has waved in the air at an invisible fly (an act of stereotypical insanity that I've only seen in movies), his narrow eyes have flitted about with a combination of paranoia and glee, and a few minutes ago, he removed from his battered satchel a battered laptop, which he has been muttering at, saying more than once: "Good to know" and "I hear you." Even the homeless have laptops in Bill Gates's hometown! And just now he went out to smoke and so I pretended to stretch and I went over and glanced at his computer screen—it's black and dead. He's a lunatic from central casting! Imaginary flies! Dead laptops!

Well, there we are. He's back now; he's not a bad guy by any means, but the fresh, acrid smell of tobacco coming through his pores is killing me. I think I'll leave. But I'm not sure what the hell I've produced over the last hour. This was supposed to be an introduction to *The Lunatic at Large* and all I've done is ramble on in some kind of knotted, nutty, self-absorbed fashion.

So I'm thinking I've got to rally at the last moment and writing something introductionish. I should mention that just before I started writing this, I read, in an e-mail, Paul Collins's foreword, and I'm not sure what comes first, an introduction or a foreword, but I'm hoping the foreword comes first since I feel like he covered the really essential stuff, and so all I'm left to say is that *I loved this book,* which, if you think about it, is your basic introduction boiled down to four words.

I don't know who I am or why what I love should have any meaning or impact, but if it does then I hope you will read this book. Then again, if you're already reading my introduction (and most people skip introductions and forewords to reissued novels), chances are you're going to read the book, unless you're reading this intro in a bookstore and you're not yet sure. For this person—and there will probably be only one of you since most people will skim the actual book in a bookstore and not the prefatory remarks, but you might have mistakenly started with my intro—I say: Read this book.

Read it right there in the bookstore if you don't have the money to purchase it. Just have fun. Have pleasure. Life is short and primarily painful, and this book is a wonderful escape and temporary antidote to that (the pain that is, not the shortness), because, you see, *The Lunatic at Large* is a dream, a delight, a joy, a gift, a love. It is a lost classic no longer lost, no longer at large, but found, right here, in your hands and before your eyes.

—*Jonathan Ames*
Seattle
October 2006

THE LUNATIC AT LARGE

INTRODUCTORY.

Into the history of Mr. Francis Beveridge, as supplied by the obliging candour of the Baron von Blitzenberg and the notes of Dr. Escott, Dr. Twiddel and his friend Robert Welsh make a kind of explanatory entry. They most effectually set the ball a-rolling, and so the story starts in a small room looking out on a very uninteresting London street.

It was about three o'clock on a November afternoon, that season of fogs and rains and mud, when townspeople long for fresh air and hillsides, and country folk think wistfully of the warmth and lights of a city, when nobody is satisfied, and everybody has a cold. Outside the window of the room there were a few feet of earth adorned with a low bush or two, a line of railings, a stone-paved street, and on the other side a long row of uniform yellow-brick houses. The apartment itself was a modest chamber, containing a minimum of rented furniture and a flickering gas-stove. By a small caseful of medical treatises and a conspicuous stethoscope, the least experienced could see that it was labelled consulting-room.

Dr. Twiddel was enjoying one of those moments of repose that occur even in the youngest practitioner's existence. For the purposes of this narrative he may briefly be described as an amiable-looking young man, with a little bit of fair moustache and still less chin, no practice to speak of, and a considerable quantity of unpaid bills. A man of such features and in such circumstances invites temptation. At the present moment, though his waistcoat was unbuttoned and his feet rested on the mantelpiece, his mind seemed not quite at ease. He looked back upon a number of fortunate events that had not occurred, and forward to various unpleasant things that might occur, and then he took a letter from his pocket and read it abstractedly.

"I can't afford to refuse," he reflected, lugubriously; "and yet, hang it! I must say I don't fancy the job."

When metal is molten it can be poured into any vessel; and at that moment a certain deep receptacle stood on the very doorstep.

The doctor heard the bell, sat up briskly, stuffed the letter back into his pocket, and buttoned his waistcoat.

"A patient at last!" and instantly there arose a vision of a simple operation, a fabulous fee, and twelve sickly millionaires an hour ever after. The door opened, and a loud voice hailed him familiarly.

"Only Welsh," he sighed, and the vision went the way of all the others.

The gentleman who swaggered in and clapped the doctor on the back, who next threw himself into the easiest chair and his hat and coat over the table, was in fact Mr. Robert Welsh. From the moment he entered he pervaded the room; the stethoscope seemed to grow less conspicuous, Dr. Twiddel's chin more diminutive, the apartment itself a mere background to this guest. Why? It would be hard to say precisely. He was a black-moustached, full-faced man, with an air of the most consummate assurance, and a person by some deemed handsome. Yet somehow or other he inevitably recalled the uncles of history. Perhaps this assurance alone gave him his atmosphere. You could have felt his egotism in the dark.

He talked in a loud voice and with a great air of mastery over all the contingencies of a life about town. You felt that here sat one who had seen the world and gave things their proper proportions, who had learned how meretricious was orthodoxy, and which bars could really be recommended. He chaffed, patronised, and cheered the doctor. Patients had been scarce, had they? Well, after all, there were many consolations. Did Twiddle say he was hard up? Welsh himself was in an even more evil case. He narrated various unfortunate transactions connected with the turf and other pursuits, with regret, no doubt, and yet with a fine rakish defiance of destiny. Twiddel's face cleared, and he began to show something of the same gallant spirit. He brought out a tall bottle with a Celtic superscription; Welsh half filled his glass, poured in some water from a dusty decanter, and proposed the toast of "Luck to the two most deserving sinners in London!"

The doctor was fired, he drew the same letter from his pocket, and cried, "By Jove, Welsh, I'd almost forgotten to tell you of a lucky offer that came this morning."

This was not strictly true, for as a matter of fact the doctor had only hesitated to tell of this offer lest he should be shamed to a decision. But Welsh was infectious.

"Congratulations, old man!" said his friend. "What's it all about?"

"Here's a letter from an old friend of my people's—Dr. Watson, by name. He has a very good country practice, and he offers me this job."

He handed the letter to Welsh, and then added, with a flutter of caution, "I haven't made up my mind yet. There are drawbacks, as you'll see."

Welsh opened the letter and read—

"DEAR TWIDDEL—I am happy to tell you that I am at last able to put something in your way. A gentleman in this neighbourhood, one of my most esteemed patients, has lately suffered from a severe mental and physical shock, followed by brain fever, and is still, I regret to say, in an extremely unstable mental condition. I have strongly recommended quiet and change of scene, and at my suggestion he is to be sent abroad under the care of a medical attendant. I have now much pleasure in offering you the post, if you would care to accept it. You will find your patient, Mr. Mandell-Essington, an extremely agreeable young man when in possession of his proper faculties. He has large means and no near relatives; he comes of one of the best families in the county; and though he has, I surmise, sown his wild oats pretty freely, he was considered of unusual promise previous to this unfortunate illness. He is of an amiable and pleasant disposition, though at present, we fear, inclined to suicidal tendencies. I have no particular reason to think he is at all homicidal; still, you will see that he naturally requires most careful watching. It is possible that you may hesitate to leave your practice (which I trust prospers); but as the responsibility is considerable, the fee will be proportionately generous—£500, and all expenses paid."

("Five hundred quid!" exclaimed Welsh.)

"I would suggest a trip on the Continent. The duration and the places to be visited will be entirely at your discretion. It is of course hardly necessary to say that you will seek quiet localities. Trusting to hear from you at your very earliest convenience, believe me, yours sincerely,

"TIMOTHY WATSON."

Welsh looked at his friend with the respect that prosperity naturally excites. He smiled on him as an equal, and cried, heartily, "Congratulations again! When do you start?"

Twiddel fidgeted uncomfortably, "I—er—well, you see—ah—I haven't *quite* made up my mind yet."

"What's the matter?"

"Hang it, Welsh—er—the fact is I don't altogether like the job."

Scruples of any kind always surprised Welsh.

"Can't afford to leave the practice?" he asked with a laugh.

"That's—ah—partly the reason," replied Twiddel, uncomfortably.

"Rot, old man! There's a girl in the case. Out with it!"

"No, it isn't that. You see it's the very devil of a responsibility."

At this confession of weakness he looked guiltily at his heroic friend. From the bottom of his heart he wished he had screwed up his courage in private. Welsh had so little imagination.

"By Gad," exclaimed Welsh, "I'd manage a nunnery for £500!"

"I daresay you would, but a suicidal, and possibly homicidal, lunatic isn't a nunnery."

Welsh looked at his friend with diminished respect.

"Then you are going to chuck up £500 and a free trip on the Continent?" he said.

"Dr. Watson himself admits the responsibility."

"With a—what is it?—agreeable young man?"

"Only when in possession of his proper faculties," said the doctor, dismally.

"And an amiable disposition?"

"With suicidal tendencies, hang it!"

"I should have thought," said Welsh, with a laugh, "that they would only matter to himself."

"But he is homicidal too—or at least it's doubtful. I want to know a little more about that, thank you!"

"What is the man's name?"

"Mandell-Essington."

"Sounds aristocratic. He might come in useful afterwards, when he's cured."

Welsh spoke with an air of reflection, which might have been entirely disinterested.

"He'd probably commit suicide first," said Twiddel, "and of course I'd get all the blame."

"Or homicide," replied Welsh, "when *he* would."

"No, he wouldn't—that's the worst of it; I'd be blamed for having my own throat cut."

"Twiddel," said his friend, deliberately, "it seems to me you're a fool."

"I'm at least alive," cried Twiddel, warming with sympathy for himself, "which I probably wouldn't be for long in Mr. Essington's company."

"I don't blame your nerves, dear boy," said Welsh, with a smile that showed all his teeth, "only your head. Here are £500 going a-begging. There must be some way—" He paused, deep in reflection. "How would it do," he remarked in a minute, "if *I* were to go in your place?"

Twiddel laughed and shook his head.

"Couldn't be managed?"

"Couldn't possibly, I'm afraid."

"No," said Welsh. "I foresee difficulties."

He fished a pipe out of his pocket, filled and lit it, and leaned back in his chair gazing at the ceiling.

"Twiddel, my boy," he said at length, "will you give me a percentage of the fee if I think of a safe dodge for getting the money and preserving your throat?"

Twiddel laughed.

"Rather!" he said.

"I am perfectly serious," replied Welsh, keenly. "I'm certain the thing is quite possible."

He half closed his eyes and ruminated in silence. The doctor watched him—fascinated, afraid. Somehow or other he felt that he was already a kind of Guy Fawkes. There was something so unlawful in Welsh's expression.

They sat there without speaking for about ten minutes, and then all of a sudden Welsh sprang up with a shout of laughter, slapping first his own leg and then the doctor's back.

"By Gad, I've got it!" he cried. "I have it!"

And he had; hence this tale.

PART I.

CHAPTER I.

In a certain fertile and well-wooded county of England there stands a high stone wall. On a sunny day the eye of the traveller passing through this province is gratified by the sparkle of myriads of broken bottles arranged closely and continuously along its coping-stone. Above these shining facets the boughs of tall trees swing in the wind and throw their shadows across the highway. The wall at last leaves the road and follows the park round its entire extent. Its height never varies; the broken bottles glitter perpetually; and only through two entrances, and that when the gates are open, can one gain a single glimpse inside: for the gates are solid, with no chinks for the curious.

The country all round is undulating, and here and there from the crest of an eminence you can see a great space of well-timbered park land within this wall; and in winter, when the leaves are off the trees, you may spy an imposing red-brick mansion in the midst.

Any native will inform you, with a mixture of infectious awe and becoming pride, that this is no less than the far-famed private asylum of Clankwood.

This ideal institution bore the enviable reputation of containing the best-bred lunatics in England. It was credibly reported that however well marked their symptoms and however well developed their delusions, none but ladies and gentlemen of the most unblemished descent were permitted to enjoy its seclusion. The dances there were universally considered the most agreeable functions in the county. The conversation of many of the inmates was of the widest range and the most refreshing originality, and the demeanour of all, even when most free from the conventional trammels of outside society, bore evidence of an expensive, and in some cases of a Christian, upbringing. This is scarcely to be wondered at, when beneath one roof were assembled the heirs-presumptive to three dukedoms, two suicidal marquises, an odd archbishop or so, and the flower of the baronetage and clergy. As this list only includes a few of the celebrities able or willing to be introduced to distinguished visitors, and makes no mention of the uncorroborated dignities (such as the classical divinities and Old Testament duplicates), the anxiety shown by some people to certify their relations can easily be understood.

Dr. Congleton, the proprietor and physician of Clankwood, was a gentleman singularly well fitted to act as host on the occasion of asylum reunions. No one could exceed him in the respect he showed to a coroneted head, even when cracked; and a bishop under his charge was always secured, as far as possible, from the least whisper of heretical conversation. He possessed besides a pleasant rubicund countenance and an immaculate wardrobe. He was further fortunate in having in his assistants, Dr. Escott and Dr. Sherlaw, two young gentlemen whose medical knowledge was almost equal to the affability of their manners and the excellence of their family connections.

One November night these two were sitting over a comfortable fire in Sherlaw's room. Twelve o'clock struck, Escott finished the remains of something in a tumbler, rose, and yawned sleepily.

"Time to turn in, young man," said he.

"I suppose it is," replied Sherlaw, a very pleasant and boyish young gentleman. "Hullo! What's that? A cab?"

They both listened, and some way off they could just pick out a sound like wheels upon gravel.

"It's very late for anyone to be coming in," said Escott.

The sound grew clearer and more unmistakably like a cab rattling quickly up the drive.

"It is a cab," said Sherlaw.

They heard it draw up before the front door, and then there came a pause.

"Who the deuce can it be?" muttered Escott.

In a few minutes there came a knock at the door, and a servant entered.

"A new case, sir. Wants to see Dr. Congleton particular."

"A man or a woman?"

"Man, sir."

"All right," growled Sherlaw. "I'll come, confound him."

"Bad luck, old man," laughed Escott. "I'll wait here in case by any chance you want me."

He fell into his chair again, lit a cigarette, and sleepily turned over the pages of a book. Dr. Sherlaw was away for a little time, and when he returned his cheerful face wore a somewhat mystified expression.

"Well?" asked Escott.

"Rather a rum case," said his colleague, thoughtfully.

"What's the matter?"

"Don't know."

"Who was it?"

"Don't know that either."

Escott opened his eyes.

"What happened, then?"

"Well," said Sherlaw, drawing his chair up to the fire again, "I'll tell you just what did happen, and you can make what you can out of it. Of course, I suppose it's all right, really, but—well, the proceedings were a little unusual, don't you know.

"I went down to the door, and there I found a four-wheeler with a man standing beside it. The door of the cab was shut, and there seemed to be two more men inside. This chap who'd got out—a youngish man—hailed me at once as though he'd bought the whole place.

" 'You Dr. Congleton?'

" 'Damn your impertinence!' I said to myself, 'ringing people up at this hour, and talking like a bally drill-sergeant.'

"I told him politely I wasn't old Congers, but that I'd make a good enough substitute for the likes of him.

" 'I tell you what it is,' said the Johnnie, 'I've brought a patient for Dr. Congleton, a cousin of mine, and I've got a doctor here, too. I want to see Dr. Congleton.'

" 'He's probably in bed,' I said, 'but I'll do just as well. I suppose he's certified, and all that.'

" 'Oh, it's all right,' said the man, rather as though he expected me to say that it wasn't. He looked a little doubtful what to do, and then I heard someone inside the cab call him. He stuck his head in the window and they confabbed for a minute, and then he turned to me and said, with the most magnificent air you ever saw, like a chap buying a set of diamond studs, 'My friend here is a great personal friend of Dr. Congleton, and it's a damned—I mean it's an uncommonly delicate matter. We must see him.'

" 'Well, if you insist, I'll see if I can get him,' I said; 'but you'd better come in and wait.'

"So the Johnnie opened the door of the cab, and there was a great hauling and pushing, my friend pulling an arm from the outside, and the doctor shoving from within, and at last they fetched out their patient. He was a tall man, in a very smart-looking, long, light top-coat, and a cap with a large peak shoved over his eyes, and he seemed very unsteady on his pins. " 'Drunk, by George!' I said to myself at first.

"The doctor—another young-looking man—hopped out after him, and they each took an arm, lugged their patient into the waiting-room, and popped him into an armchair. There he collapsed, and sat with his head hanging down as limp as a sucked orange.

"I asked them if anything was the matter with him.

" 'Only tired—just a little sleepy,' said the cousin.

"And do you know, Escott, what I'd stake my best boots was the matter with him?"

"What?"

"The man was drugged!"

Escott looked at the fire thoughtfully.

"Well," he said, "it's quite possible; he might have been too violent to manage."

"Why couldn't they have said so, then?"

"H'm. Not knowing, can't say. What happened next?"

"Next thing was, I asked the doctor what name I should give. He answered in a kind of nervous way, 'No name; you needn't give any name. I know Dr. Congleton personally. Ask him to come, please.' So off I tooled, and found old Congers just thinking of turning in.

" 'My clients are sometimes unnecessarily discreet,' he remarked in his pompous way when I told him about the arrival, and of course he added his usual platitude about our reputation for discretion.

"I went back with him to the waiting-room, and just stood at the door long enough to see him hail the doctor chap very cordially and be introduced to the patient's cousin, and then I came away. Rather rum, isn't it?"

"You've certainly made the best of the yarn," said Escott with a laugh.

"By George, if you'd been there you'd have thought it funny too."

"Well, good-night, I'm off. We'll probably hear tomorrow what it's all about."

But in the morning there was little more to be learned about the newcomer's history and antecedents. Dr. Congleton spoke of the matter to the two young men, with the pompous cough that signified extreme discretion.

"Brought by an old friend of mine," he said. "A curious story, Escott, but quite intelligible. There seem to be the best reasons for answering no questions about him; you understand?"

"Certainly, sir," said the two assistants, with the more assurance as they had no information to give.

"I am perfectly satisfied, mind you—perfectly satisfied," added their chief.

"By the way, sir," Sherlaw ventured to remark, "hadn't they given him something in the way of a sleeping-draught?"

"Eh? Indeed? I hardly think so, Sherlaw, I hardly think so. Case of reaction entirely. Good morning."

"Congleton seems satisfied," remarked Escott.

"I'll tell you what," said the junior, profoundly. "Old Congers is a very good chap, and all that, but he's not what I should call extra sharp. *I* should feel uncommon suspicious."

"H'm," replied Escott. "As you say, our worthy chief is not extra sharp. But that's not our business, after all."

CHAPTER II.

"By the way," said Escott, a couple of days later, "how is your mysterious man getting on? I haven't seen him myself yet."

Sherlaw laughed.

"He's turning out a regular sportsman, by George! For the first day he was more or less in the same state in which he arrived. Then he began to wake up and ask questions. 'What the devil is this place?' he said to me in the evening. It may sound profane, but he was very polite, I assure you. I told him, and he sort of raised his eyebrows, smiled, and thanked me like a Prime Minister acknowledging an obligation. Since then he has steadily developed sporting, not to say frisky, tastes. He went out this morning, and in five minutes had his arm round one of the prettiest nurses' waist. And she didn't seem to mind much either, by George!"

"He'll want a bit of looking after, I take it."

"Seems to me he is uncommonly capable of taking care of himself. The rest of the establishment will want looking after, though."

From this time forth the mysterious gentleman began to regularly take the air and to be remarked, and having once remarked him, people looked again.

Mr. Francis Beveridge, for such it appeared was his name, was distinguished even for Clankwood. Though his antecedents were involved in mystery, so much confidence was placed in Dr. Congleton's discrimination that the unknown stranger was at once received on the most friendly terms by everyone; and, to tell the truth, it would have been hard to repulse him for long. His manner was perfect, his conversation witty to the extremest verge of propriety, and his clothes, fashionable in cut and of unquestionable fit, bore on such of the buttons as were made of metal the hallmark of a leading London firm. He wore the longest and most silky moustaches ever seen, and beneath them a short well-tended beard completed his resemblance—so the ladies declared—to King Charles of unhappy memory. The melancholic Mr. Jones (quondam author of "Sunflowers—A Lyrical Medley") declared, indeed, that for Mr. Beveridge shaving was prohibited, and darkly whispered "suicidal," but his opinion was held of little account.

It was upon a morning about a week after his arrival that Dr. Escott, alone in the billiard-room, saw him enter. Escott had by this time made his acquaintance, and, like almost everybody else, had already succumbed to the fascination of his address.

"Good morning, doctor," he said; "I wish you to do me a trifling favour, a mere bending of your eyes."

Escott laughed.

"I shall be delighted. What is it?"

Mr. Beveridge unbuttoned his waistcoat and displayed his shirt-front.

"I only want you to be good enough to read the inscription written here."

The doctor bent down.

" 'Francis Beveridge,' " he said. "That's all I see."

"And that's all I see," said Mr. Beveridge. "Now what can you read here? I am not troubling you?"

He held out his handkerchief as he spoke.

"Not a bit," laughed the doctor, "but I only see 'Francis Beveridge' here too, I'm afraid."

"Everything has got it," said Mr. Beveridge, shaking his head, it would be hard to say whether humorously or sadly. "'Francis Beveridge' on everything. It follows, I suppose, that I am Francis Beveridge?"

"What else?" asked Escott, who was much amused.

"That's just it. What else?" said the other. He smiled a peculiarly charming smile, thanked the doctor with exaggerated gratitude, and strolled out again.

"He is a rum chap," reflected Escott.

And indeed in the outside world he might safely have been termed rather rum, but here in this backwater, so full of the oddest flotsam, his waywardness was rather less than the average. He had, for instance, a diverting habit of modifying the time, and even the tune, of the hymns on Sunday, and he confessed to having kissed all the nurses and housemaids except three. But both Escott and Sherlaw declared they had never met a more congenial spirit. Mr. Beveridge's game of billiards was quite remarkable even for Clankwood, where the enforced leisure of many of the noblemen and gentlemen had made them highly proficient on the spot; he showed every promise, on his rare opportunities, of being an unusually entertaining small-hour, whisky-and-soda *raconteur*; in fact, he was evidently a man whose previous career, whatever it might have been (and his own statements merely served to increase the mystery round this point), had led him through many humorous by-paths, and left him with few restrictive prejudices.

November became December, and to all appearances he had settled down in his new residence with complete resignation, when that unknowable factor that upsets so many calculations came upon the scene—the factor, I mean, that wears a petticoat.

Mr. Beveridge strolled into Escott's room one morning to find the doctor inspecting a mixed assortment of white kid gloves.

"Do these mean past or future conquests?" he asked with his smile.

"Both," laughed the doctor. "I'm trying to pick out a clean pair for the dance tonight."

"You go a-dancing, then?"

"Don't you know it's our own monthly ball here?"

"Of course," said Mr. Beveridge, passing his hand quickly across his brow. "I must have heard, but things pass so quickly through my head nowadays."

He laughed a little conventional laugh, and gazed at the gloves.

"You are coming, of course?" said Escott.

"If you can lend me a pair of these. Can you spare one?"

"Help yourself," replied the doctor.

Mr. Beveridge selected a pair with the care of a man who is particular in such matters, put them in his pocket, thanked the doctor, and went out.

"Hope he doesn't play the fool," thought Escott.

Invitations to the balls at Clankwood were naturally in great demand throughout the county, for nowhere were noblemen so numerous and divinities so tangible. Carriages and pairs rolled up one after another, the mansion glittered with lights, the strains of the band could be heard loud and stirring or low and faintly all through the house.

"Who is that man dancing opposite my daughter?" asked the Countess of Grillyer.

"A Mr. Beveridge," replied Dr. Congleton.

Mr. Beveridge, in fact, the mark of all eyes, was dancing in a set of lancers. The couple opposite to him consisted of a stout elderly gentleman who, doubtless for the best reasons, styled himself the Emperor of the two Americas, and a charming little pink and flaxen partner—the Lady Alicia à Fyre, as everybody who was anybody could have told you. The handsome stranger moved, as might be expected, with his accustomed grace and air of distinction, and, probably to convince his admirers that there was nothing meretricious in his performance, he carried his hands in his pockets the whole time. This certainly caused a little inconvenience to his partner, but to be characteristic in Clankwood one had to step very far out of the beaten track.

For two figures the Emperor snorted disapproval, but at the end of the third, when Mr. Beveridge had been skipping round the outskirts of the set, his hands still thrust out of sight, somewhat to the derangement of the customary procedure, he could contain himself no longer.

"Hey, young man!" he asked in his most stentorian voice, as the music ceased, "are you afraid of having your pockets picked?"

"Alas!" replied Mr. Beveridge, "it would take two men to do that."

"Huh!" snorted the Emperor, "you are so d—d strong, are you?"

"I mean," answered his *vis-à-vis* with his polite smile, "that it would take one man to put something in and another to take it out."

This remark not only turned the laugh entirely on Mr. Beveridge's side, but it introduced the upsetting factor.

CHAPTER III.

The Lady Alicia à Fyre, though of the outer everyday world herself, had, in common with most families of any pretensions to ancient dignity, a creditable sprinkling of uncles and cousins domiciled in Clankwood, and so she frequently attended these dances.

Tonight her eye had been caught by a tall, graceful figure executing a *pas seul* in the middle of the room with its hands in its pockets. The face of this gentleman was so composed and handsome, and he seemed so oblivious to the presence of everybody else, that her interest was immediately excited. During the set of lancers in which he was her *vis-à-vis* she watched him furtively with a growing feeling of admiration. She had never heard him say a word, and it was with a sensation of the liveliest interest that she listened to his brief passage with her partner. At his final retort her tender heart was overcome with pity. He was poor, then, or at least he was allowed the use of no money. And all of him that was outside his pockets seemed so sane and so gentlemanly; it seemed a pity to let him lack a little sympathy.

The Lady Alicia might be described as a becoming frock stuffed with sentiment. Through a pair of large blue eyes she drank in romance, and with the reddest and most undecided of lips she felt a vague desire to kiss something. At the end of the dance she managed by a series of little manoeuvres to find herself standing close to his elbow. She sighed twice, but he still seemed absorbed in his thoughts. Then with a heroic effort she summed up her courage, and said in a low and rather shaky voice, "You—you—you are unha—appy."

Mr. Beveridge turned and looked down on her with great interest. Her eyes met his for a moment and straightway sought the floor. Thus she saw nothing of a smile that came and went like the shadow of a puff of smoke. He took his hands out of his pockets, folded his arms, and, with an air of the deepest dejection, sighed heavily. She took courage and looked up again, and then, as he only gazed into space in the most romantically melancholy fashion and made no answer, she asked again very timidly, "Wh—what is the matter?"

Without saying a word Mr. Beveridge bent courteously and offered her his right arm. She took it with the most delicious trepidation, glancing round hurriedly to see whether the Countess noticed her. Another dance was just beginning, and in the general movement her mysterious acquaintance led her without observation to a seat in the window of a corridor. There he pressed her hand gently, stroked his long moustaches for a minute, and then said, with an air of reflection: "There are three ways of making a woman like one. I am slightly out of practice. Would you be kind enough to suggest a method of procedure?"

Such a beginning was so wholly unexpected that Lady Alicia could only give a little gasp of consternation. Her companion, after pausing an instant for a reply, went on in the same tone, "I am aware that I have begun well. I attracted your attention, I elicited your sympathy, and I pressed your hand; but for the life of me I can't remember what I generally do next."

Poor Lady Alicia, who had come with a bucketful of sympathy ready to be gulped down by this unfortunate gentleman, was only able to stammer, "I—I really don't know, Mr.—"

"Hamilton," said Mr. Beveridge, unblushingly. "At least that name belongs to me as much as anything can be said to in a world where my creditors claim my money and Dr. Congleton my person."

"You are confined and poor, you mean?" asked Lady Alicia,

beginning to see her way again.

"Poor and confined, to put them in their proper order, for if I had the wherewithal to purchase a balloon I should certainly cease to be confined."

His admirer found it hard to reply adequately to this, and Mr. Beveridge continued, "To return to the delicate subject from which we strayed, what would you like me to do—put my arm round your waist, relate my troubles, or turn my back on you?"

"Are—are those the three ways you spoke of—to make women like you, I mean?" Lady Alicia ventured to ask, though she was beginning to wish the sofa was larger.

"They are examples of the three classical methods: cuddling, humbugging, and piquing. Which do you prefer?"

"Tell me about your—your troubles," she answered, gaining courage a little.

"You belong to the sex which makes no mention of figs and spades," he rejoined; "but I understand you to mean that you prefer humbugging."

He drew a long face, sighed twice, and looking tenderly into Lady Alicia's blue eyes, began in a gentle, reminiscent voice, "My boyhood was troubled and unhappy: no kind words, no caresses. I was beaten by a cruel stepfather, ignored and insulted for my physical deformities by a heartless stepmother."

He stopped to sigh again, and Lady Alicia, with a boldness that surprised herself, and a perspicacity that would have surprised her friends, asked, "How could they—I mean, were they *both* step?"

"Several steps," he replied; "in fact, quite a long journey."

With this explanation Lady Alicia was forced to remain satisfied; but as he had paused a second time, and seemed to be immersed in the study of his shoes, she inquired again, "You spoke of physical infirmities; do you mean—?"

"Deformities," he corrected; "up to the age of fourteen years I could only walk sideways, and my hair parted in the middle."

He spoke so seriously that these unusual maladies seemed to her the most touching misfortunes she had ever heard of. She murmured gently, "Yes?"

"As the years advanced," Mr. Beveridge continued, "and I became more nearly the same weight as my stepfather, my life grew happier. It was decided to send me to college, so I was provided with an insufficient cheque, a complete set of plated forks, and three bath-towels, and despatched to the University of Oxford. At least I think that was the name of the corporation which took my money and endeavoured to restrict my habits, though, to confess the truth, my memory is not what it used to be. There I learned wisdom by the practice of folly—the most amusing and effective method. My tutor used to tell me I had some originality. I apologised for its presence in such a respectable institution, and undertook to pass an examination instead. I believe I succeeded: I certainly remember giving a dinner to celebrate something. Thereupon at my own expense the University inflicted a degree upon me, but I was shortly afterwards compensated by the death of my uncle and my accession to his estates. Having enjoyed a university education, and accordingly possessing a corrected and regulated sentiment, I was naturally inconsolable at the decease of this venerable relative, who for so long had shown a kindly interest in the poor orphan lad."

He stopped to sigh again, and Lady Alicia asked with great interest, "But your stepparents, you always had them, hadn't you?"

"Never!" he replied, sadly.

"Never?" she exclaimed in some bewilderment.

"Certainly not often," he answered, "and oftener than not, never. If you had told me beforehand you wished to hear my history, I should have pruned my family tree into a more presentable shape. But if you will kindly tell me as I go along which of my relatives you disapprove of, and who you would like to be introduced, I shall arrange the plot to suit you."

"I only wish to hear the true story, Mr. Hamilton."

"Fortescue," he corrected. "I certainly prefer to be called by one name at a time, but never by the same twice running."

He smiled so agreeably as he said this that Lady Alicia, though puzzled and a little hurt, could not refrain from smiling back.

"Let me hear the rest," she said.

"It is no truer than the first part, but quite as entertaining. So, if you like, I shall endeavour to recall the series of painful episodes that brought me to Clankwood," he answered, very seriously. Lady Alicia settled herself comfortably into one corner of the sofa and prepared to feel affected. But at that moment the portly form of Dr. Congleton appeared from the direction of the ballroom with a still more portly dowager on his arm.

"My mother!" exclaimed Lady Alicia, rising quickly to her feet.

"Indeed?" said Mr. Beveridge, who still kept his seat. "She certainly looks handsome enough."

This speech made Lady Alicia blush very becomingly, and the Countess looked at her sharply.

"Where have you been, Alicia?"

"The room was rather warm, mamma, and—"

"In short, madam," interrupted Mr. Beveridge, rising and bowing, "your charming daughter wished to study a lunatic at close quarters. I am mad, and I obligingly raved. Thus—" He ran one hand through his hair so as to make it fall over his eyes, blew out his cheeks, and uttering a yell, sprang high into the air, and descended in a sitting posture on the floor.

"That, madam, is a very common symptom," he explained, with a smile, smoothing down his hair again, "as our friend Dr. Congleton will tell you."

Both the doctor and the Countess were too astonished to make any reply, so he turned again to Lady Alicia, and offering his arm, said, "Let me lead you back to our fellow-fools."

"Is he safe?" whispered the Countess.

"I—I believe so," replied Dr. Congleton in some confusion; "but I shall have him watched more carefully."

As they entered the room Mr. Beveridge whispered, "Will you meet a poor lunatic again?" And the Lady Alicia pressed his arm.

CHAPTER IV.

On the morning after the dance Dr. Congleton summoned Dr. Escott to his room.

"Escott," he began, "we must keep a little sharper eye on Mr. Beveridge."

"Indeed, sir?" said Escott; "he seems to me harmless enough."

"Nevertheless, he must be watched. Lady Grillyer was considerably alarmed by his conduct last night, and a client who has confided so many of her relatives to my care must be treated with the greatest regard. I receive pheasants at Christmas from no fewer than fourteen families of title, and my reputation for discretion is too valuable to be risked. When Mr. Beveridge is not under your own eyes you must see that Moggridge always keeps him in sight."

Accordingly Moggridge, a burly and seasoned attendant on refractory patients, was told off to keep an unobtrusive eye on that accomplished gentleman. His duties appeared light enough, for, as I have said, Mr. Beveridge's eccentricities had hitherto been merely of the most playful nature.

After luncheon on this same day he gave Escott twelve breaks and a beating at billiards, and then having borrowed and approved of one of his cigars, he strolled into the park. If he intended to escape observation, he certainly showed the most skillful strategy, for he dodged deviously through the largest trees, and at last, after a roundabout ramble, struck a sheltered walk that ran underneath the high, glass-decked outer wall. It was a sunny winter afternoon. The boughs were stripped, and the leaves lay littered on the walk or flickered and stirred through the grass. In this spot the high trees stood so close and the bare branches were so thick that there was still an air of quiet and seclusion where he paced and smoked. Every now and then he stopped and listened and looked at his watch, and as he walked backwards and forwards an amused smile would come and go.

All at once he heard something move on the far side of the wall: he paused to make sure, and then he whistled. The sounds outside ceased, and in a moment something fell softly behind him. He turned quickly and snatched up a little buttonhole of flowers with a still smaller note tied to the stems.

"An uncommonly happy idea," he said to himself, looking at the missive with the air of one versed in these matters. Then he leisurely proceeded to unfold and read the note.

"To my friend," he read, "if I may call you a friend, since I have known you only *such a short time*—may I? This is just to express my sympathy, and although I cannot express it well, still perhaps you will forgive my feeble effort!!"

At this point, just as he was regarding the double mark of exclamation with reminiscent entertainment, a plaintive voice from the other side of the wall cried in a stage whisper, "Have you got it?"

Mr. Beveridge composed his face, and heaving his shoulders to his ears in the effort, gave vent to a prodigious sigh.

"A million thanks, my fairest and kindest of friends," he answered in the same tone. "I read it now: I drink it in, I—"

He kissed the back of his hand loudly two or three times, sighed again, and continued his reading.

"I wish I could help you," it ran, "but I am afraid I cannot, as the world is so *censorious,* is it not? So you must accept a friend's sympathy if it does not seem to you too bold and forward of her!!! Perhaps we may meet again, as I sometimes go to Clankwood. *Au revoir.*—Your sympathetic well-wisher. A. À. F."

He folded it up and put it in his waistcoat-pocket, then he exclaimed in an audible aside, his voice shaking with the most affecting thrill, "*Perhaps* we may meet again! Only *perhaps!* O Alicia!" And then dropping again into a stage whisper, he asked, "Are you still there, Lady Alicia?"

A timorous voice replied, "Yes, Mr. Fortescue. But I really *must* go now!"

"Now? So soon?"

"I have stayed too long already."

" 'Tis better to have stayed too long than never to wear stays at all," replied Mr. Beveridge.

There was no response for a moment. Then a low voice, a little hurt and a good deal puzzled, asked with evident hesitation, "What—what did you say, Mr. Fortescue?"

"I said that Lady Alicia's stay cannot be too long," he answered, softly.

"But—but what good can I be?"

"The good you cannot help being."

There was another moment's pause, then the voice whispered, "I don't quite understand you."

"My Alicia understands me not!" Mr. Beveridge soliloquised in another audible aside. Aloud, or rather in a little lower tone, he answered, "I am friendless, poor, and imprisoned. What is the good in your staying? Ah, Lady Alicia! But why should I detain you? Go, fair friend! Go and forget poor Francis Beveridge!"

There came a soft, surprised answer, "Francis Beveridge?"

"Alas! you have guessed my secret. Yes, that is the name of the unhappiest of mortals."

As he spoke these melancholy words he threw away the stump of his cigar, took another from his case, and bit off the end.

The voice replied, "I shall remember it—among my friends."

Mr. Beveridge struck a match.

"H'sh! Whatever is that?" cried the voice in alarm.

"A heart breaking," he replied, lighting his cigar.

"Don't talk like that," said the voice. "It—it distresses me." There was a break in the voice.

"And, alas! between distress and consolation there are fifteen perpendicular feet of stone and mortar and the relics of twelve hundred bottles of Bass," he replied.

"Perhaps,"—the voice hesitated—"perhaps we may see each other someday."

"Say tomorrow at four o'clock," he suggested, pertinently. "If you could manage to be passing up the drive at that hour."

There was another pause.

"Perhaps—" the voice began.

At that moment he heard the sharp crack of a branch behind him, and turning instantly he spied the uncompromising countenance of Moggridge peering round a tree about twenty paces distant. Lack of presence of mind and quick decision were not amongst Mr. Beveridge's failings. He struck a theatrical attitude at once, and began in a loud voice, gazing up at the tops of the trees, "He comes! A stranger comes! Yes, my fair friend, we may meet again. *Au revoir,* but only for a while! Ah, that a breaking heart should be lit for a moment and then the lamp be put out!"

Meanwhile Moggridge was walking towards him.

"Ha, Moggridge!" he cried. "Good day."

"Time you was goin' in, sir," said Moggridge, stolidly; and to himself he muttered, "He's crackeder than I thought, a-shoutin' and a-ravin' to hisself. Just as well I kept a heye on 'im."

Like most clever people, Mr. Beveridge generally followed the line of least resistance. He slipped his arm through his attendant's, shouted a farewell apparently to some imaginary divinity overhead, and turned towards the house.

"This is an unexpected pleasure," he remarked.

"Yes, sir," replied Moggridge.

"Funny thing your turning up. Out for a walk, I suppose?"

"For a stroll, sir—that's to say—" he stopped.

"That on these chilly afternoons the dear good doctor is afraid of my health?"

"That's kind o' it, sir."

"But of course I'm not supposed to notice anything, eh?"

Moggridge looked a trifle uncomfortable and was discreetly silent. Mr. Beveridge smiled at his own perspicacity, and then began in the most friendly tone, "Well, I feel flattered that so stout a man has been told off to take care of me. What an arm you've got, man."

"Pretty fair, sir," said Moggridge, complacently.

"And I am thankful, too," continued Mr. Beveridge, "that you're a man of some sense. There are a lot of fools in the world, Moggridge, and I'm somewhat of an epicure in the matter of heads."

"Mine 'as been considered pretty sharp," Moggridge admitted, with a gratified relaxation of his wooden countenance.

"Have a cigar?" his patient asked, taking out his case.

"Thank you, sir, I don't mind if I do."

"You will find it a capital smoke. I don't throw them away on everyone."

Moggridge, completely thawed, lit his cigar and slackened his pace, for such frank appreciation of his merits was rare in a critical world.

"You can perhaps believe, Moggridge," said Mr. Beveridge, reflectively, "that one doesn't often have the chance of talking confidentially to a man of sense in Clankwood."

"No, sir, I should himagine not."

"And so one has sometimes to talk to oneself."

This was said so sadly that Moggridge began to feel uncomfortably affected.

"Ah, Moggridge, one cannot always keep silence, even when one least wants to be overheard. Have you ever been in love, Moggridge?"

The burly keeper changed countenance a little at this embarrassingly direct question, and answered diffidently, "Well, sir, to be sure men is men and woming will be woming."

"The deuce, they will!" replied Mr. Beveridge, cordially; "and it's rather hard to forget 'em, eh?"

"Hindeed it is, sir."

"I remembered this afternoon, but I should like you as a good chap to forget. You won't mention my moment of weakness, Moggridge?"

"No, sir," said Moggridge, stoutly. "I suppose I hought to report what I sees, but I won't this time."

"Thank you," said Mr. Beveridge, pressing his arm. "I had, you know, a touch of the sun in India, and I sometimes talk when I shouldn't. Though, after all, that isn't a very uncommon complaint."

And so it happened that no rumour prejudicial either to his sanity or to the progress of his friendship with the Lady Alicia reached the ears of the authorities.

CHAPTER V.

Towards four o'clock on the following afternoon Mr. Beveridge and Moggridge were walking leisurely down the long drive leading from the mansion of Clankwood to the gate that opened on the humdrum outer world. Finding that an inelastic matter of yards was all the tether he could hope for, Mr. Beveridge thought it best to take the bull by the horns, and make a companion of this necessity. So he kept his attendant by his side, and regaled him for some time with a series of improbable reminiscences and tolerable cigars, till at last, round a bend of the avenue, a lady on horseback came into view. As she drew a little nearer he stopped with an air of great surprise and pleasure.

"I believe, Moggridge, that must be Lady Alicia à Fyre!" he exclaimed.

"It looks huncommon like her, sir," replied Moggridge.

"I must really speak to her. She was"—and Mr. Beveridge assumed his inimitable air of manly sentiment—"she was one of my poor mother's dearest friends. Do you mind, Moggridge, falling behind a little? In fact, if you could step behind a tree and wait here for me, it would be pleasanter for us both. We used to meet under happier circumstances, and, don't you know, it might distress her to be reminded of my misfortunes."

Such a reasonable request, beseechingly put by so fine a gentleman, could scarcely be refused. Moggridge retired behind the trees that lined the avenue, and Mr. Beveridge advanced alone to meet the Lady Alicia. She blushed very becomingly as he raised his hat.

"I hardly expected to see you today, Mr. Beveridge," she began.

"I, on the other hand, have been thinking of nothing else," he replied.

She blushed still deeper, but responded a little reprovingly, "It's very polite of you to say so, but—"

"Not a bit," said he. "I have a dozen equally well-turned sentences at my disposal, and, they tell me, a most deluding way of saying them."

Suddenly out of her depth again, poor Lady Alicia could only strike out at random.

"Who tell you?" she managed to say.

"First, so far as my poor memory goes, my mother's lady's-maid informed me of the fact; then I think my sister's governess," he replied, ticking off his informants on his fingers with a half-abstracted air. "After that came a number of more or less reliable individuals, and lastly the Lady Alicia à Fyre."

"Me? I'm sure I never said—"

"None of them ever *said,*" he interrupted.

"But what have I done, then?" she asked, tightening her reins, and making her horse fidget a foot or two farther away.

"You have begun to be a most adorable friend to a most unfortunate man."

Still Lady Alicia looked at him a little dubiously, and only said, "I—I hope I'm not too friendly."

"There are no degrees in friendly," he replied. "There are only aloofly, friendly, and more than friendly."

"I—I think I ought to be going on, Mr. Beveridge."

That experienced diplomatist perceived that it was necessary to further embellish himself.

"Are you fond of soldiers?" he asked, abruptly.

"I beg your pardon?" she said in considerable bewilderment.

"Does a red coat, a medal, and a brass band appeal to you? Are you apt to be interested in her Majesty's army?"

"I generally like soldiers," she admitted, still much surprised at the turn the conversation had taken.

"Then I was a soldier."

"But—really?"

"I held a commission in one of the crackest cavalry regiments," he began dramatically, and yet with a great air of sincerity. "I was considered one of the most promising officers in the mess. It nearly broke my heart to leave the service."

He turned away his head. Lady Alicia was visibly affected.

"I am so sorry!" she murmured.

Still keeping his face turned away, he held out his hand and she pressed it gently.

"Sorrow cannot give me my freedom," he said.

"If there is anything I can do—" she began.

"Dismount," he said, looking up at her tenderly.

Lady Alicia never quite knew how it happened, but certainly she found herself standing on the ground, and the next moment Mr. Beveridge was in her place.

"An old soldier," he exclaimed, gaily; "I can't resist the temptation of having a canter." And with that he started at a gallop towards the gate.

With a blasphemous ejaculation Moggridge sprang from behind his tree, and set off down the drive in hot pursuit.

Lady Alicia screamed, "Stop! stop! Francis—I mean, Mr. Beveridge; stop, please!"

But the favourite of the crack regiment, despite the lady's saddle, sat his steed well, and rapidly left cries and footsteps far behind. The lodge was nearly half a mile away, and as the avenue wound between palisades of old trees, the shouts became muffled, and when he looked over his shoulder he saw in the stretch behind him no sign of benefactress or pursuer. By continued exhortations and the point of his penknife he kept his horse at full stretch; round the next bend he knew he should see the gates.

"Five to one on the blank things being shut," he muttered.

He swept round the curve, and there ahead of him he saw the gates grimly closed, and at the lodge door a dismounted groom, standing beside his horse.

Only remarking "Damn!" he reined up, turned, and trotted quietly back again. Presently he met Moggridge, red in the face, muddy as to his trousers, and panting hard.

"Nice little nag this, Moggridge," he remarked, airily.

"Nice sweat you've give me," rejoined his attendant, wrathfully.

"You don't mean to say you ran after me?"

"I does mean to say," Moggridge replied grimly, seizing the reins.

"Want to lead him? Very well—it makes us look quite like the Derby winner coming in."

"Derby loser you means, thanks to them gates bein' shut."

"Gates shut? Were they? I didn't happen to notice."

"No, o' course not," said Moggridge, sarcastically; "that there sunstroke you got in India prevented you, I suppose?"

"Have a cigar?"

To this overture Moggridge made no reply. Mr. Beveridge laughed and continued lightly, "I had no idea you were so fond of exercise. I'd have given you a lead all round the park if I'd known."

"You'd 'ave given me a lead all round the county if them gates 'ad been open."

"It might have been difficult to stop this fiery animal," Mr. Beveridge admitted. "But now, Moggridge, the run is over. I think I can take Lady Alicia's horse back to her myself."

Moggridge smiled grimly.

"You won't let go?"

"No fears."

Mr. Beveridge put his hand behind his back and silently drove the penknife a quarter of an inch into his mount's hind quarters. In an instant his keeper felt himself being lifted nearly off his feet, and in another actually deposited on his face. Off went the accomplished horseman again at top speed, but this time back to Lady Alicia. He saw her standing by the side of the drive, her handkerchief to her eyes, a penitent and disconsolate little figure. When she heard him coming, she dried her eyes and looked up, but her face was still tearful.

"Well, I am back from my ride," he remarked in a perfectly usual voice, dismounting as he spoke.

"The man!" she cried, "where is that dreadful man?"

"What man?" he asked in some surprise.

"The man who chased you."

Mr. Beveridge laughed aloud, at which Lady Alicia took fresh refuge in her handkerchief.

"He follows on foot," he replied.

"Did he catch you? Oh, why didn't you escape altogether?" she sobbed.

Mr. Beveridge looked at her with growing interest.

"I had begun to forget my petticoat psychology," he reflected (aloud, after his unconventional fashion).

"Oh, here he comes," she shuddered. "All blood! Oh, what have you done to him?"

"On my honour, nothing—I merely haven't washed his face."

By this time Moggridge was coming close upon them.

"You won't forget a poor soldier?" said Mr. Beveridge in a lower voice.

There was no reply.

"A *poor* soldier," he added, with a sigh, glancing at her from the corner of his eye. "So poor that even if I had got out, I could only have ridden till I dropped."

"Would you accept—?" she began, timidly.

"What day?" he interrupted, hurriedly.

"Tuesday," she hesitated.

"Four o'clock, again. Same place as before. When I whistle throw it over at once."

Before they had time to say more, Moggridge, blood- and gravel-stained, came up.

"It's all right, miss," he said, coming between them; "I'll see that he plays no more of 'is tricks. There's nothin' to be afrightened of."

"Stand back!" she cried; "don't come near me!"

Moggridge was too staggered at this outburst to say a word.

"Stand away!" she said, and the bewildered attendant stood away. She turned to Mr. Beveridge.

"Now, will you help me up?"

She mounted lightly, said a brief farewell, and, forgetting all about the call at Clankwood she had ostensibly come to pay, turned her horse's head towards the lodge.

"Well, I'm blowed!" said Moggridge.

"They do blow one," his patient assented.

Naturally enough the story of this equestrian adventure soon ran through Clankwood. The exact particulars, however, were a little hard to collect, for while Moggridge supplied many minute and picturesque details, illustrating his own activity and presence of mind and the imminent peril of the Lady Alicia, Mr. Beveridge recounted an equally vivid story of a runaway horse recovered by himself to its fair owner's unbounded gratitude. Official opinion naturally accepted the official account, and for the next few days Mr. Beveridge became an object of considerable anxiety and mistrust.

"I can't make the man out," said Sherlaw to Escott. "I had begun to think there was nothing much the matter with him."

"No more there is," replied Escott. "His memory seems to me to have suffered from something, and he simply supplies its place in conversation from his imagination, and in action from the inspiration of the moment. The methods of society are too orthodox for such an aberration, and as his friends doubtless pay a handsome fee to keep him here, old Congers labels him mad and locks the door on him."

A day or two afterwards official opinion was a little disturbed. Lady Alicia, in reply to anxious inquiries, gave a third version of the adventure, from which nothing in particular could be gathered except that nothing in particular had happened.

"What do you make of this, Escott?" asked Dr. Congleton, laying her note before his assistant.

"Merely that a woman wrote it."

"Hum! I suppose that *is* the explanation."

Upon which the doctor looked profound and went to lunch.

CHAPTER VI.

"Two five-pound notes, half-a-sovereign, and seven and sixpence in silver," said Mr. Beveridge to himself. "Ah, and a card."

On the card was written, "From a friend, if you will accept it. A."

He was standing under the wall, in the secluded walk, holding a little lady's purse in his hand, and listening to two different footsteps. One little pair of feet were hurrying away on the farther side of the high wall, another and larger were approaching him at a run.

"Wot's he bin up to now, I wonder," Moggridge panted to himself—for the second pair of feet belonged to him. "Shamming nosebleed and sending me in for an 'andkerchief, and then sneaking off here by 'isself!"

"What a time you've been," said Mr. Beveridge, slipping the purse with its contents into his pocket. "I was so infernally cold I had to take a little walk. Got the handkerchief?"

In silence and with a suspicious solemnity Moggridge handed him the handkerchief, and they turned back for the house.

"Now for a balloon," Mr. Beveridge reflected.

Certainly it was cold. The frost nipped sharp that night, and next morning there were ice gardens on the windows, and the park lay white all through the winter sunshine.

By evening the private lake was reported to be bearing, and the next day it hummed under the first skaters. Hardly necessary to say Mr. Beveridge was among the earliest of them, or that he was at once the object of general admiration and envy. He traced "vines" and "Q's," and performed wonderful feats on one leg all morning. At lunch he was in the best of spirits, and was off again at once to the ice.

When he reached the lake in the afternoon the first person he spied was Lady Alicia, and five minutes afterwards they were sailing off together hand in hand.

"I knew you would come today," he remarked.

"How *could* you have known? It was by the merest chance I happened to come."

"It has always been by the merest chance that any of them have ever come."

"Who have ever come?" she inquired, with a vague feeling that he had said something he ought not to have, and that she was doing the same.

"Many things," he smiled, "including purses. Which reminds me that I am eternally your debtor."

She blushed and said, "I hope you didn't mind."

"Not much," he answered, candidly. "In my present circumstances a five-pound note is more acceptable than a caress."

The Lady Alicia again remembered the maidenly proprieties, and tried to change the subject.

"What beautiful ice!" she said.

"The question now is," he continued, paying no heed to this diversion, "what am I to do next?"

"What do you mean?" she asked a little faintly, realising dimly that she was being regarded as a fellow-conspirator in some unlawful project.

"The wall is high, there is bottle-glass on the top, and I shall find it hard to bring away a fresh pair of trousers, and probably draughty if I don't. The gates are always kept closed, and it isn't worth anyone's while to open them for £10, 17s. 6d., less the price of a first-class ticket up to town. What are we to do?"

"We?" she gasped.

"You and I," he explained.

"But—but I can't *possibly* do anything."

" 'Can't possibly' is a phrase I have learned to misunderstand."

"Really, Mr. Beveridge, I mustn't do anything."

"Mustn't is an invariable preface to a sin. Never use it; it's a temptation in itself."

"It wouldn't be right," she said, with quite a show of firmness.

He looked at her a little curiously. For a moment he almost seemed puzzled. Then he pressed her hand and asked tenderly, "Why not?"

And in a half-audible aside he added, "That's the correct move, I think."

"What did you say?" she asked.

"I said, 'Why not?' " he answered, with increasing tenderness.

"But you said something else."

"I added a brief prayer for pity."

Lady Alicia sighed and repeated a little less firmly. "It wouldn't be right of me, Mr. Beveridge."

"But what would be wrong?"

This was said with even more fervour.

"My conscience—we are very particular, you know."

"Who are 'we'?"

"Papa is *very* strict High Church."

An idea seemed to strike Mr. Beveridge, for he ruminated in silence.

"I asked Mr. Candles—our curate, you know," Lady Alicia continued, with a heroic effort to make her position clear.

"You told him!" he exclaimed.

"Oh, I didn't say who it was—I mean what it was I thought of doing—I mean the temptation—that is, the possibility. And he said it was very kind of me to think of it; but I mustn't do anything, and he advised me to read a book he gave me, and—and I mustn't think of it, really, Mr. Beveridge."

To himself Mr. Beveridge repeated under his breath, "Archbishops, bishops, deacons, curates, fast in Lent, and an anthem after the Creed. I think I remember enough to pass."

Then he assumed a very serious face, and said aloud, "Your scruples do your heart credit. They have given me an insight into your deep and sweet character, which emboldens me to make a confession."

He stopped skating, folded his arms, and continued unblushingly, "I was educated for the Church, but the prejudices of my parents, the immature scepticism of youth, and some uncertainty about obtaining my archbishopric, induced me in an unfortunate moment, which I never ceased to bitterly regret, to quit my orders."

"You are in orders?" she exclaimed.

"I was in several. I cancelled them, and entered the Navy instead."

"The Navy?" she asked, excusably bewildered by these rapid changes of occupation.

"For five years I was never ashore."

"But," she hesitated—"but you said you were in the Army."

Mr. Beveridge gave her a look full of benignant compassion that made her, she did not quite know why, feel terribly abashed.

"My regiment was quartered at sea," he condescended to explain. "But in time my conscience awoke. I announced my intention of resuming my charge. My uncle was furious. My enemies were many. I was seized, thrown into this prison-house, and now my only friend fails me."

They were both silent. She ventured once to glance up at his face, and it seemed to her that his eyes were moist—though perhaps it was that her own were a little dim.

"Let us skate on," he said abruptly, with a fine air of resignation.

"By the way," he suddenly added, "I was extremely High Church, in fact almost freezingly high."

For five minutes they skated in silence, then Lady Alicia began softly, "Supposing you—you went away—"

"What is the use of talking of it?" he exclaimed, melodramatically. "Let me forget my short-lived hopes!"

"You *have* a friend," she said, slowly.

"A friend who tantalises me by 'supposings'!"

"But supposing you did, Mr. Beveridge, would you go back to your—did you say you had a parish?"

"I had: a large, populous, and happy parish. It is my one dream to sit once more on its council and direct my curate."

"Of course that makes a difference. Mr. Candles didn't know all this."

They had come by this time to the corner of a little island that lay not far from the shore; in the channel ahead a board labelled "Danger" marked a hidden spring; behind them the shining ice was almost bare of skaters, for all but Dr. Escott seemed to be leaving; on the bank they could see Moggridge prowling about in the gathering dusk, a vigilant reminder of captivity. Mr. Beveridge took the whole scene in with, it is to be feared, a militant rather than an episcopal eye. Then he suddenly asked, "Are you alone?"

"Yes."

"You drive back?"

"Ye-es."

He took out his watch and made a brief calculation.

"Go now, call at Clankwood or do anything else you like, and pass down the drive again at a quarter to five."

This sudden pinning of her irresolution almost took Lady Alicia's breath away.

"But I never said—" she began.

"My dear friend," he interrupted, "in the hour of action only a fool ever says. Come on."

And while she still hesitated they were off again.

"But—" she tried to expostulate.

"My dearest friend," he whispered, "and my dear old vicarage!"

He gave her no time to protest. Her skates were off, she was on her way to her carriage, and he was striking out again for the middle of the lake before she had time to collect her wits.

He took out his watch and looked at the time. It was nearly a quarter-past four. Then he came up to Escott, who by this time was the only other soul on the ice.

"About time we were going in," said Escott.

"Give me half-an-hour more. I'll show you how to do that vine you admired."

"All right," assented the doctor.

A minute or two later Mr. Beveridge, as if struck by a sudden reflection, exclaimed, "By Jove, there's that poor devil Moggridge freezing to death on shore. Can't you manage to look after so dangerous a lunatic yourself? It is his tea-time, too."

"Hallo, so he is," replied Escott; "I'll send him up."

And so there were only left the two men on the ice.

For a little the lesson went on, and presently, leaving the doctor to practise, Mr. Beveridge skated away by himself. He first paused opposite a seat on the bank over which hung Dr. Escott's great fur coat. This spectacle appeared to afford him peculiar pleasure. Then he looked at his watch. It was half-past four. He shut the watch with a click, threw a glance at his pupil, and struck out for the island. If the doctor had been looking, he might have seen him round it in the gloaming.

Dr. Escott, leaning far on his outside edge, met him as he returned.

"What's that under your coat?" he asked.

"A picture I intend to ask your opinion on presently," replied Mr. Beveridge; and he added, with his most charming air, "But now, before we go in, let me give you a ride on one of these chairs, doctor."

They started off, the pace growing faster and faster, and presently Dr. Escott saw that they were going behind the island.

"Look out for the spring!" he cried.

"It must be bearing now," replied Mr. Beveridge, striking out harder than ever; "they have taken away the board."

"All right," said the doctor, "on you go."

As he spoke he felt a violent push, and the chair, slewing round as it went, flew on its course unguided. Mr. Beveridge's skates rasped on the ice with a spray of white powder as he stopped himself suddenly. Ahead of him there was a rending crack, and Dr. Escott and his chair disappeared. Mr. Beveridge laughed cheerfully, and taking from under his coat a board with the legend "Danger" printed in large characters across its face, he placed it beside the jagged hole.

"Here is the picture, doctor," he said, as a dripping, gasping head came up for the second time. "I must ask a thousand pardons for this—shall I say, liberty? But, as you know, I'm off my head. Good night. Let me recommend a hot drink when you come out. There are only five feet of water, so you won't drown." And with that he skated rapidly away.

Escott had a glimpse of him vanishing round the corner of the island, and then the ice broke again, and down he went. Four, five, six times he made a desperate effort to get out, and every time the thin ice tore under his hands, and he slipped back again. By the seventh attempt he had broken his way to the thicker sheet; he got one leg up, slipped, got it up again, and at last, half numbed and wholly breathless, he was crawling circumspectly away. When at last he ventured to rise to his feet, he skated with all the speed he could make to the seat where he had left his coat. A pair of skates lay there instead, but the coat had vanished. Dr. Escott's philosophical estimate of Mr. Beveridge became considerably modified.

"Thank the Lord, he can't get out of the grounds," he said to himself; "what a dangerous devil he is! But he'll be sorry for this performance, or I'm mistaken."

When he arrived at the house his first inquiries were for his tutor in the art of vine-cutting, and he was rather surprised to hear that he had not yet returned, for he only imagined himself the victim of a peculiarly ill-timed practical joke.

Men with lanterns were sent out to search the park; and still there was no sign of Mr. Beveridge. Inquiries were made at the lodge, but the gatekeeper could swear that only a single carriage had passed through. Dr. Congleton refused at first to believe that he could possibly have got out.

"Our arrangements are perfect—the thing's absurd," he said, peremptorily.

"That there man, sir," replied Moggridge, who had been summoned, "is the slipperiest customer as ever I seed. 'E's hout, sir, I believe."

"We might at least try the stations," suggested Escott, who had by this time changed, and indulged in the hot drink recommended.

The doctor began to be a little shaken.

"Well, well," said he, "I'll send a man to each of the three stations within walking distance; and whether he's out or in, we'll have him by tomorrow morning. I've always taken care that he had no money in his pockets."

But what is a doctor's care against a woman's heart? For many tomorrows Clankwood had to lament the loss of the gifted Francis Beveridge.

CHAPTER VII.

At sixteen minutes to five Mr. Beveridge stood by the side of the Clankwood Avenue, comfortably wrapped in Dr. Escott's fur coat, and smoking with the greatest relish one of Dr. Escott's undeniable cigars.

It was almost dark, the air bit keen, the dim park with its population of black trees was filled with a frosty, eager stillness. All round the invisible wall hemmed him in, the ten pounds, seventeen shillings, and sixpence lay useless in his pocket till that was past, and his one hope depended on a woman. But Mr. Beveridge was an amateur in the sex, and he smiled complacently as he smoked.

He had waited barely three minutes when the quick clatter of a pair of horses fell on his ears, and presently the lights of a carriage and pair, driving swiftly away from Clankwood, raked the drive on either side. As they rattled up to him he gave a shout to the coachman to stop, and stepped right in front of the horses. With something that sounded unlike a blessing, the pair were thrown almost on their haunches to check them in time. Never stopping to explain, he threw open the door and sprang in; the coachman, hearing no sound of protest, whipped up again, and Mr. Beveridge found himself rolling through the park of Clankwood in the Countess of Grillyer's carriage with a very timid little figure by his side. Even in that moment of triumphant excitement the excellence of his manners was remarkable: the first thing he said was, "Do you mind smoking?"

In her confusion of mind Lady Alicia could only reply "Oh no," and not till some time afterwards did she remember that the odour of a cigar was clinging and the Countess's nose unusually sensitive.

After this first remark he leaned back in silence, gradually filling the carriage with a blue-grey cloud, and looking out of the windows first on one side and then on the other. They passed quickly through the lines of trees and the open spaces of frosty park-land, they drew up at the lodge for a moment, he heard his prison gates swing open, the harness jingled and the hoofs began to clatter again, a swift vision of lighted windows and a man looking on them incuriously swept by, and then they were rolling over a country road between hedgerows and under the free stars.

It was the Lady Alicia who spoke first.

"I never thought you would really come," she said.

"I have been waiting for that remark," he replied, with his most irresistible smile; "now for some more practical conversation."

As he did not immediately begin this conversation himself, her curiosity overcame her, and she asked, "How did you manage to get out?"

"As my friend Dr. Escott offered no opposition, I walked away."

"Did he really let you?"

"He never even expostulated."

"Then—then it's all right?" she said, with an inexplicable sensation of disappointment.

"Perfectly—so far."

"But—didn't they object?"

"Not yet," he replied; "objections to my movements are generally made after they have been performed."

Somehow she felt immensely relieved at this hint of opposition.

"I'm so glad you got away," she whispered, and then repented in a flutter.

"Not more so than I am," he answered, pressing her hand.

"And now," he added, "I should like to know how near Ashditch Junction you propose to take me."

"Where are you going to, Mr. Beveridge?"

The "Mr. Beveridge" was thrown in as a corrective to the hand-pressure.

"To London; where else, my Alicia? With £10, 17s. 6d. in my pocket, I shall be able to eat at least three good dinners, and, by the third of them, if I haven't fallen on my feet it will be the first time I have descended so unluckily."

"But," she asked, considerably disconcerted, "I thought you were going back to your parish."

For a moment he too seemed a trifle put about. Then he replied readily, "So I am, as soon as I have purchased the necessary outfit, restocked my ecclesiastical library, and called on my bishop."

She felt greatly relieved at this justification of her share in the adventure.

"Drop me at the nearest point to the station," he said.

"I am afraid," she began—"I mean I think you had better get out soon. The first road on the right will take you straight there, and we had better not pass it."

"Then I must bid you farewell," and he sighed most effectively. "Farewell, my benefactress, my dear Alicia! Shall I ever see you, shall I ever hear of you again?"

"I might—I might just write once; if you will answer it: I mean if you would care to hear from such a—"

She found it difficult to finish, and prudently stopped.

"Thanks," he replied cheerfully; "do—I shall live in hopes. I'd better stop the carriage now."

He let down the window, when she said hastily, "But I don't know your address."

He reflected for an instant. "Care of the Archbishop of York will always find me," he replied; and as if unwilling to let his emotion be observed, he immediately put his head out of the window and called on the coachman to stop.

"Good-bye," he whispered, tenderly, squeezing her fingers with one hand and opening the door with the other.

"Don't quite forget me," she whispered back.

"Never!" he replied, and was in the act of getting out when he suddenly turned, and exclaimed, "I must be more out of practice than I thought; I had almost forgotten the protested salute."

And without further preamble the Lady Alicia found herself kissed at last.

He jumped out and shut the door, and the carriage with its faint halo clattered into the darkness.

"They are wonderfully alike," he reflected.

About twenty minutes later he walked leisurely into Ashditch Junction, and having singled out the station-master, he accosted him with an air of beneficient consideration and inquired how soon he could catch a train for London.

It appeared that the up express was not due for nearly three-quarters of an hour.

"A little too long to wait," he said to himself, as he turned up the collar of his purloined fur coat to keep out the cold, and picked another cigar from its rightful owner's case.

By way of further defying the temperature and cementing his acquaintance with the station-master, he offered to regale that gratified official with such refreshments as the station bar provided. In the consumption of whiskies-and-sodas (a beverage difficult to obtain in any quantity at Clankwood) Mr. Beveridge showed himself as accomplished as in every other feat. In thirty-five minutes he had despatched no fewer than six, besides completely winning the station-master's heart. As he had little more than five minutes now to wait, he bade a genial farewell to the lady behind the bar, and started to purchase his ticket.

Hardly had he left the door of the refreshment-room when he perceived an uncomfortably familiar figure just arrived, breathless with running, on the opposite platform. The light of a lamp fell on his shining face: it was Moggridge!

A stout heart might be forgiven for sinking at the sight, but Mr. Beveridge merely turned to his now-firm friends and said with his easiest air, "On the opposite platform I perceive one of my runaway lunatics. Bring a couple of stout porters as quickly as you can, for he is a person of much strength and address. My name," he drew a card-case from the pocket of his fur coat, "is, as you see, Dr. Escott of Clankwood."

Meanwhile Moggridge, after hurriedly investigating the platform he was on, suddenly spied a tall fur-coated figure on the opposite side. Without a moment's hesitation he sprang onto the rails, and had just mounted the other side as the station-master and two porters appeared.

Seeing his allies by his side Mr. Beveridge never said a word, but, throwing off his hat, he lowered his head, charged his keeper, and picking him up by the knees threw him heavily on his back. Before he had a chance of recovering himself the other three were seated on his chest employed in winding a coil of rope round and round his prostrate form.

Two minutes later Moggridge was sitting bound hand and foot in the booking office, addressing an amused audience in a strain of perhaps excusable exasperation, which however merely served to impress the Ashditch officials with a growing sense of their address in capturing so dangerous a lunatic. In the middle of this entertaining scene the London express steamed in, and Mr. Beveridge, courteously thanking the station-master for his assistance, stepped into a first-class carriage.

"I should be much obliged," he said, leaning on the door of his compartment and blowing the smoke of Dr. Escott's last Havannah lightly from his lips, "if you would be kind enough to keep that poor fellow in the station till tomorrow. It is rather too late to send him back now. Good night, and many thanks."

He pressed a coin into the station-master's hand, which that disapponted official only discovered on emptying his pockets at night to be an ordinary sixpence, the guard whistled, and one by one, smoothly and slowly and then in a bright stream, the station lamps slipped by. The last of them flitted into the night, and the train swung and rattled by a mile a minute nearer to London town and farther from the high stone wall. There was no other stop, and for a long hour the adventurer sat with his legs luxuriously stretched along the cushions looking out into a fainter duplicate of his carriage, pierced now and then by the glitter of brighter points as they whisked by some wayside village, or crossed by the black shadows of trees. The whole time he smiled contentedly, doubtless at the prospect of his parish work. All at once he seemed stirred, and, turning in his seat, laid his face upon the window, and pulled down the blind behind his head, so that he could see into the night. He had spied the first bright filaments of London. Quickly they spread into a twinkling network, and then as quickly were shut out by the first line of suburb houses; through the gaps they grew nearer and flared cheerfully; the train hooted over an archway, and in the road below he had a glimpse of shop windows and crowded pavements and moving omnibuses: he was in the world again, and at the foretaste of all this life he laughed like a delighted child. Last of all came the spread of shining rails and the red and yellow lights of many signals, and then the high glass roof and long lamp-lit platforms of St Euston's Cross.

Unencumbered by luggage or plans, Mr. Francis Beveridge stuck his hands deep in his pockets and strolled aimlessly enough out of the station into the tideway of the Euston Road. For a little he stood stock-still on the pavement watching the throng of people and the perpetual buses and drays and the jingling hansoms picking their way through it all.

"For a man of brains," he moralised, "even though he be certified as insane, for probably the best of reasons, this London has surely fools enough to provide him with all he needs and more than he deserves. I shall set out with my lantern like a second Diogenes to look for a foolish man."

And so he strolled along again to the first opening southwards. That led him through a region of dingy enough brick by day, but decked now with its string of lamps and bright shop-windows here and there, and kept alive by passing buses and cabs going and coming from the station. Farther on the street grew gloomier, and a dark square with a grove of trees in the middle opened off one side; but, rattle or quiet, flaring shops or sad-looking lodgings, he found it all too fresh and amusing to hurry.

"Back to my parish again," he said to himself, smiling broadly at the drollery of the idea. "If I'm caught tomorrow, I'll at least have one merry night in my wicked, humorous old charge."

He reached Holborn and turned west in the happiest and most enviable of moods; the very policemen seemed to cast a friendly eye on him; the frosty air, he thought, made the lights burn brighter and the crowd move more briskly than ever he had seen them. Suddenly the sight of a hairdresser's saloon brought an inspiration. He stroked his beard, twisted his moustaches half regretfully, and then exclaiming, "Exit Mr. Beveridge," turned into the shop.

PART II.

CHAPTER I.

The Baron Rudolf von Blitzenberg sat by himself at a table in the dining-room of the Hôtel Mayonaise, which, as everybody knows, is the largest and most expensive in London. He was a young man of a florid and burly Teutonic type and the most ingenuous countenance. Being possessed of a curious and enterprising disposition, as well as the most ample means, he had left his ancestral castle in Bavaria to study for a few months the customs and politics of England. In the language he was already proficient, and he had promised himself an amusing as well as an instructive visit. But, although he had only arrived in London that morning, he was already beginning to feel an uncomfortable apprehension lest in both respects he should be disappointed. Though his introductions were the best with which the British Ambassador could supply him, they were only three or four in number—for, not wishing to be hampered with too many acquaintances, he had rather chosen quality than quantity: and now, in the course of the afternoon, he had found to his chagrin that in every case the families were out of town. In fact, so far as he could learn, they were not even at their own country seats. One was abroad, another gone to the seaside to recover from the mumps, and a third paying a round of visits.

The disappointment was sharp, he felt utterly at sea as to what he should do, and he was already beginning to experience the loneliness of a single mortal in a crowded hotel.

As the frosty evening was setting in and the shops were being lit, he had strolled out into the streets in the vague hope of meeting some strange foreign adventure, or perhaps even happily lighting upon some half-forgotten diplomatic acquaintance. But he found the pavements crowded with a throng who took no notice of him at all, but seemed every man and most women of them to be pushing steadily, and generally silently, towards a million mysterious goals. Not that he could tell they were silent except by their set lips, for the noise of wheels and horses on so many hundreds of miles of streets, and the cries of busmen and vendors of evening papers, made such a hubbub that he felt before long in a maze. He lost his way four times, and was patronisingly set right by beneficent policemen; and at last, feeling like a man who has fallen off a precipice onto a soft place—none the worse but quite bewildered—he struggled back to his hotel. There he spun out his time by watching the people come and go, and at last dressed with extra deliberation.

About eight o'clock he sat down to his solitary dinner. The great gilt and panelled room was full of diners and bustling waiters, but there was not a face the Baron had ever seen before. He was just finishing a plate of whitebait when he observed a stranger enter the room and stroll in a very self-possessed manner down the middle, glancing at the tables round him as though he was looking either for a friend or a desirable seat. This gentleman was tall, fair, and clean-shaved; he was dressed in a suit of well-fitting tweeds, and his air impressed the Baron as being natural and yet distinguished. At last his eye fell upon the Baron, who felt conscious of undergoing a quick, critical scrutiny. The table at which that nobleman sat was laid for two, and coming apparently to a sudden resolution, the good-looking stranger seated himself in the vacant chair. In an agreeable voice and with an unmistakably well-bred air he asked a waiter for the wine-list, and then, like a man with an excellent appetite, fell upon the various *hors d'oeuvres,* the entire collection of which, in fact, he consumed in a wonderfully short space of time. The Baron, being himself no trifler with his victuals, regarded this feat with sympathetic approval, and began to feel a little less alone in the world. His naturally open disposition was warmed besides, owing to a slight misconception he had fallen into, perfectly excusable however in a foreigner. He thought he had read somewhere that port was the usual accompaniment to the first courses of an English dinner, and as his waiter had been somewhat dilatory in bringing him the more substantial items of the repast, he had already drunk three claret-glasses of this cheering wine. The chill recollections of his sixteen quarterings and the exclusiveness he had determined to maintain as becoming to his rank were already melting, and he met the stranger's eye with what for the life of him he could not help being a cordial look.

His *vis-à-vis* caught the glance, smiled back, and immediately asked, with the most charming politeness, "Do you care, sir, to split a bottle of champagne?"

"To—er—*shplid*?" said the Baron, with a disappointed consciousness of having been put at a loss in his English by the very first man who had spoken to him.

"I beg your pardon—I am afraid I was unintelligibly idiomatic. To divide, I should say, you consuming one-half, I the other. Am I clear, sir?"

For a moment the Baron was a little taken aback, and then recollecting that the dining habits of the English were still new to him, he concluded that the suggestion was probably a customary act of courtesy. He had already come to the conclusion that the gentleman must be a person of rank, and he replied affably, "Yah—zat is, vid pleasure. Zanks, very."

"The pleasure is mine," said the stranger—"and half the bottle," he added, smiling.

The Baron, whose perception of humour had been abnormally increased by this time, laughed hilariously at the infection of his new acquaintance's smile.

"Goot, goot!" he cried. "Ach, yah, zo."

"Am I right, sir, in supposing that, despite the perfection of your English accent, I cannot be fortunate enough to claim you as a countryman?" asked the stranger.

The Baron's resolutions of reticence had vanished altogether before such unexpected and (he could not but think) un-English friendliness. He unburdened his heart with a rush.

"You have ze right. I am Deutsch. I have gom to England zis day for to lairn and to amuse myself. But mein, vat you call?—introdogtions zey are not inside, gat is zey are from off. Not von, all, every single gone to ze gontry or to abroad. I am alone, I eat my dinner in zolitude, I am pleased to meet you, sare."

A cork popped and the champagne frothed into the stranger's glass. Raising it to his lips, he said, "Prosit!"

"Prosit!" responded the Baron, enthusiastically. "You know ze Deutsch, sare?"

"I am safer in English, I confess."

"Ach, das ist goot, I vant for to practeese. Ve vill talk English."

"With all my heart," said the stranger. "I, too, am alone, and I hold myself more than fortunate in making your acquaintance. It's a devilish dull world when one can't share a bottle—or a brace of them, for the matter of that."

"You know London?" asked the Baron.

"I used to, and I daresay my memory will revive."

"I know it not, pairhaps you can inform. I haf gom, as I say, today."

"With pleasure," said the stranger, readily. "In fact, if you are ever disengaged I may possibly be able to act as showman."

"Showman!" roared the Baron, thinking he had discovered a jest. "Ha, ha, ha! Goot, zehr goot!"

The other looked a trifle astonished for an instant, and then as he sipped his champagne an expression of intense satisfaction came over his face.

"I can put away my lantern," he said to himself—"I have found him."

"May I have the boldness to ask your name, sir?" he asked aloud.

"Ze Baron Rudolph von Blitzenberg," that nobleman replied. "Yours, sare—may I dare?"

"Francis Bunker, at your service, Baron."

"You are noble?" queried the Baron a little anxiously, for his prejudices on this point were strong.

"According to your standard I believe I may say so. That's to say, my family have borne arms for two hundred odd generations; twenty-five per cent of them have died of good living; and the most malicious have never accused us of brains. I myself may not be very typical, but I assure you it isn't my ancestors' fault."

The latter part of this explanation entirely puzzled the Baron. The first statement, though eminently satisfactory, was also a little bewildering.

"Two hondred generations?" he asked, courteously. "Zat is a vary old family. All bore arms you say, Mistair Bonker?"

"All," replied Mr. Bunker, gravely. "The first few bore tails as well."

"Ha, ha, ha!" laughed the Baron. "You are a fonny man I pairceive, vat you call clown, yes?"

"What my friends call clown, and I call wit," Mr. Bunker corrected.

"Vit! Ha, ha, ha!" roared the Baron, whose mind was now in an El Dorado of humour where jokes grew like daisies. His loneliness had disappeared as if by magic; as course succeeded course his contentment showed itself in a perpetually beaming smile: he ceased to worry even about his friend's pedigree, convinced in his mind that manners so delightful and distinguished could only result from repeated quarterings and unoccupied forefathers. Yet by the time dessert arrived and he had again returned to his port, he began to feel an extreme curiosity to know more concerning Mr. Bunker. He himself had volunteered a large quantity of miscellaneous information: about Bavaria, its customs and its people, more especially the habits and history of the Blitzenberg family; about himself, his parentage and education; all about his family ghost, his official position as hereditary carpet-beater to the Bavarian Court, and many other things equally entertaining and instructive. Mr. Bunker, for his part, had so far confined his confidences to his name.

"My dear Bonker," said the Baron at last—he had become quite familiar by this time—"vat make you in London? I fear you are bird of passage. Do you stay long?"

Mr. Bunker cracked a nut, looking very serious; then he leant on one elbow, glanced up at the ceiling pensively, and sighed.

"I hope I do not ask vat I should not," the Baron interposed, courteously.

"My dear Baron, ask what you like," replied Mr. Bunker. "In a city full of strangers, or of friends who have forgotten me, you alone have my confidence. My story is a common one of youthful folly and present repentance, but such as it is, you are welcome to it."

The Baron gulped down half a glass of port and leaned forward sympathetically.

"My father," Mr. Bunker continued with an air of half-sad reminiscence, "is one of the largest landowners and the head of one of the most ancient families in the north of England. I was his eldest son and heir. I am still, I have every reason to believe, his eldest son, but my heirship, I regret to say, is more doubtful. I spent a prodigal youth and a larger sum of money than my poor father approved of. He was a strict though a kind parent, and for the good of my health and the replenishment of the family coffers, which had been sadly drained by my extravagance, he sent me abroad. There I have led a roving life for the last six years, and at last, my wild oats sown, reaped, and gathered in (and a well-filled stockyard they made, I can assure you), I decided to return to England and become an ornament to respectable society. Like you, I arrived in London today, but only to find to my disgust that my family have gone to winter in Egypt. So you see that at present I am like a ship-wrecked sailor clinging to a rock and waiting, with what patience I can muster, for a boat to take me off."

"You mean," inquired the Baron, anxiously, "that you vish to go to Egypt at vonce?"

"I had thought of it; though there is a difficulty in the way, I admit."

"You vill not stay zen here?"

"My dear Baron, why should I? I have neither friends nor—"

He stopped abruptly.

"I do not like to zink I shall lose your company so soon."

"I admit," allowed Mr. Bunker, "that this fortunate meeting tempts me to stay."

"Vy not?" said the Baron, cordially. "Can your fader not vait to see you?"

"I hardly think he will worry about me, I confess."

"Zen stay, my goot Bonker!"

"Unfortunately there is the same difficulty as stands in the way of my going to Egypt."

"And may I inquire vat zat is?"

"To tell you the truth," replied Mr. Bunker, with an air of reluctant candour, "my funds are rather low. I had trusted to finding my father at home, but as he isn't, why—" he shrugged his shoulders and threw himself back in his chair.

The Baron seemed struck with an idea which he hesitated to express.

"Shall we smoke?" his friend suggested.

"Vaiter!" cried the Baron, "bring here two best cigars and two coffee!"

"A liqueur, Baron?"

"Ach, yah. Vat for you?"

"A liqueur brandy suggests itself."

"Vaiter! And two brandy."

"And now," said the Baron, "I haf an idea, Bonker."

CHAPTER II.

The Baron Rudolph von Blitzenberg, as I have said, had a warm heart. He was, besides, alone in one hundred and twenty square miles of strangers and foreigners when he had happened upon this congenial spirit. He began in a tone of the most ingenuous friendliness—

"I haf no friends here. My introdogtions zey are gone. Bot I haf moch money, and I vish a, vat you say?—showman, ha, ha, ha! You haf too leetle money and no friends and you can show. You show and I will loan you vat you vish. May I dare to suggest?"

"My dear Baron!"

"My goot Bonker! I am in airnest, I assure. Vy not? It is vun gentleman and anozzer."

"You are far too kind."

"It is to myself I am kind, zen. I vant a guide, a frient. It is a loan. Do not scruple. Ven your fader goms you can pay if you please. It is nozing to me."

"Well, my dear Baron," said Mr. Bunker, like a man persuaded against his will, "what can I say? I confess I might find a little difficulty in replenishing my purse without resorting to disagreeable means, and if you really wish my society, why—"

"Zen it is a bairgain?" cried the Baron.

"If you insist—"

"I insist. Vaiter! Alzo two ozzer liqueur. Ve most drink to ze bairgain, Bonker."

They pledged each other cordially, and talked from that moment like old friends. The Baron was thoroughly pleased with himself, and Mr. Bunker seemed no less gratified at his own good fortune. Half an hour went quickly by, and then the Baron exclaimed, "Let us do zomzing tonight, Bonker. I burn for to begin zis show of London."

"What would you care to do, Baron? It is rather late, I am afraid, to think of a theatre. What do you say to a music-hall?"

"Music-hall? I haf seen zem at home. Damned amusing, das ist ze expression, yes?"

"It is a perfect description."

"Bot," continued the Baron, solemnly, "I must not begin vid ze vickedest."

"And yet," replied his friend, persuasively, "even wickedness needs a beginning."

"Bot, if I begin I may not stop. Zomzing more qviet ze first night. Haf you a club?"

Mr. Bunker pondered for a moment, and a curious smile stole across his face. Then it vanished, and he answered readily, "Certainly, Baron, an excellent idea. I haven't been to my club for so long that it never struck me. Let us come."

"Goot!" cried the Baron, rising with alacrity.

They put on their coats (Mr. Bunker's, it may be remarked, being a handsome fur-lined garment), the porter hailed a cab, and the driver was ordered to take them to the Regent's Club in Pall Mall. The Baron knew it by reputation as the most exclusive in London, and his opinion of his friend rose still higher.

They joined a jingling string of other hansoms and sped swiftly through the exhilarating bustle of the streets. To the Baron it seemed as if a great change had come over the city since he wandered disconsolately before dinner. Carried swiftly to the music of the little bells through the sharp air and the London night that is brighter than day, with a friend by his side and a good dinner within, he marked the most astonishing difference. All the people seemed to talk and laugh, and for his own part he found it hard to keep his tongue still.

"I know ze name of ze Regent's," he said; "vun club of ze best, is it not?"

"The very best club, Baron."

"Zey are all noble?"

"In many cases the receipts for their escutcheons are still in their pockets."

Though the precise significance of this explanation was not quite clear to the Baron, it sounded eminently satisfactory.

"Zo?" he said. "I shall be moch interested to see zem."

As they entered the club the porter stared at them curiously, and even made a movement as though he would step out and address them; but Mr. Bunker, wishing him a courteous good evening, walked briskly up to the hat-and-cloak racks in the hall. A young man had just hung up his hat, and as he was divesting himself of his coat, Mr. Bunker quickly took the hat down, glanced at the name inside, and replaced it on its peg. Then he held out his hand and addressed the young man cordially.

"Good evening, Transome, how are you?" said he, and, heedless of the look of surprise on the other's face, he turned towards the Baron and added, "Let me introduce the Baron Rudolph von Blitzenberg—Mr. Transome. The Baron has just come to England, and I thought he couldn't begin better than by a visit to the Regent's. Let us come into the smoking-room."

In a few minutes they were all on the best of terms. A certain perplexity, and almost shyness, that the young man showed at first, vanished rapidly before the Baron's cordiality and Mr. Bunker's well-bred charm of manner.

They were deeply engrossed in a discussion on the reigning sovereign of the Baron's native land, a monarch of whose enlightened policy that nobleman spoke with pardonable pride, when two elderly gentlemen entered the room.

"Who are these?" Mr. Bunker whispered to Transome. "I know them very well, but I am always bad at names."

"Lord Fabrigas and General M'Dermott," replied Transome.

Instantly Mr. Bunker rose and greeted the newcomers.

"Good evening, Lord Fabrigas; good evening, General. You have just come in time to be introduced to the Baron Rudolph von Blitzenberg, whom you doubtless know by reputation."

The Baron rose and bowed, and it struck him that elderly English gentlemen were singularly stiff and constrained in their manner. Mr. Bunker, however, continued cheerfully, "We are just going to have a smoking concert. Will you begin, Baron?"

"I know not English songs," replied the Baron, "bot I should like moch to hear."

"You must join in the chorus, then."

"Certainly, Bonker. I haf a voice zat is considered—vat you call—deafening, yes?—in ze chorus."

Mr. Bunker cleared his throat, and, just as the General was on the point of interposing a remark, struck up hastily; and for the first time in its long and honourable history the smoking-room of the Regent's Club re-echoed to a popular music-hall ditty.

"They sometimes call 'em duckies, they sometimes call 'em pets,
And sometimes they refer to 'em as dears,
They live on little matters that a gentleman forgets,
In a little world of giggles and of tears;
There are different varieties from which a man may choose,
There are sorts and shapes and sizes without end,
But the kind I'd pick myself is the kind you introduce
By the simple title of 'my lady friend.' "

"Chorus, Baron!" And then he trolled in waltz time this edifying refrain—

"My lady friend, my lady friend!

Can't you twig, dear boys,
From the sound of the kisses
She isn't my misses,
She's only my lady friend!"

In a voice like a train going over a bridge the Baron chimed in—

"My laty vrient, my laty vrient!
Cannot you tvig, mine boy
Vrom ze sound of ze kiss
He is not my miss
He is only mine laty vrient!"

"I am afraid," said Mr. Bunker, as they finished the chorus, "that I can't remember any more. Now, General, it's your turn."

"Sir," replied that gallant officer, who had listened to this ditty in purple and petrified astonishment, "I don't know who the devil you are, but I can tell you, you won't remain a member of this club much longer if you come into it again in this state."

"I had forgotten," said Mr. Bunker, with even more than his usual politeness, "that such an admirable music-hall critic was listening to me. I must apologise for my poor effort."

Wishing him courteously good-night, he took the Baron by the arm and walked out. While that somewhat perplexed nobleman was struggling into his coat, his friend rapidly and dexterously converted all the silk hats he could see into the condition of collapsed opera hats, and then picked a small hand-bag off the floor. The Baron walked out through the door first, but Mr. Bunker stopped for an instant opposite the hall-porter's box, and crying, "Good night to you, sir!" hurled the bag through the glass, rushed after his friend, and in less time than it takes to tell they were tearing up Pall Mall in a hansom.

For a few minutes both were silent; then the Baron said slowly, "I do not qvite onderstand."

"My dear Baron," his friend explained gaily, "these practical jokes are very common in our clubs. They are quite part of our national life, you know, and I thought you ought to see everything."

The Baron said nothing, but he began to realise that he was indeed in a foreign country.

CHAPTER III.

"Vell, Bonker, vat show today?" said the Baron.

Mr. Bunker sipped his coffee and smiled back at his friend.

"What would you like?" said he.

They were sitting in the Baron's private room finishing one of the renowned Hôtel Mayonaise breakfasts. Out of the windows they could see the bright curving river, the bare tops of the Embankment trees, a file of barges drifting with the tide, and cold-looking clouds hurrying over the chaos of brick on the opposite shore. It was a bright breezy morning, and the Baron felt in high good-humour with his surroundings. On maturer consideration, the entertaining experience of the night before had greatly raised Mr. Bunker in his estimation. He had chuckled his way through a substantial breakfast, and in such good company felt ready for any adventure that might turn up.

He lit a cigar, pushed back his chair, and replied blandly, "I am in your hands. I am ready to enjoy anyzing."

"Do you wish instruction or entertainment?"

"Mix zem, Bonker. Entertain by instrogtion; instrogt by entertaining."

"You are epigrammatic, Baron, but devilish vague. I presume, however, that you wish entertaining experience from which a man of your philosophical temperament can draw a moral—afterwards."

"Ha, ha!" laughed the Baron. "Excellent! You provide ze experiences—I draw ze moral."

"And we share the entertainment. The theory is perfect, but I'm afraid we need a programme. Now, on my own first visit to London I remember being taken—by the hand—to Madame Tussaud's Waxworks, the Tower, St Paul's Cathedral, the fishmarket at Billingsgate, the British Museum, and a number of other damnably edifying spectacles. You might naturally suppose that after such a round it would be quite superfluous for me ever to come up to town again. Yet, surprising as it may appear, most of the knowledge of London I hope to put at your disposal has been gained in the course of subsequent visits."

"Bot zese places—Tousaud, Tower, Paul's—are zey not instrogtif?"

"If you wish to learn that a great number of years ago a vast quantity of inconsequent events occurred, or that in an otherwise amusing enough world there are here and there collected so many roomfuls of cheerless articles, I can strongly recommend a visit to the Tower of London or the British Museum."

"In mine own gontry," said the Baron, thoughtfully, "I can lairn zo moch."

"Then, my dear Baron, while you are here forget it all."

"And yet," said the Baron, still thoughtfully, "somzing I should lairn here."

"Certainly; you will learn something of what goes on underneath a waistcoat and a little of the contents of a corset and petticoat. Also of the strange customs of this city and the excellence of British institutions."

"Ha, ha, ha!" laughed the Baron, who thought that if his friend had not actually made a jest, it was at least time for one to occur. "I see, I see. I draw ze moral, ha, ha!"

"This morning," Mr. Bunker continued, reflectively, "we might—let me see—well, we might do a little shopping. To tell you the truth, Baron, my South African experiences have somewhat exhausted my wardrobe."

"Ach, zo. Cairtainly ve vill shop. Bot, Bonker, Soud Africa? Vas it not Soud America?"

"Did I say Africa? America of course I meant. Well, let us shop if you have no objections: then we might have a little lunch, and afterwards visit the Park. For the evening, what do you say to a theatre?"

"Goot!" cried the Baron. "Make it tzos."

Mr. Bunker's shopping turned out to be a pretty extensive operation.

"Loan vat you please of money," said his friend. "A gentleman should be dressed in agreement."

With now and then an apology for his extravagance, he took full advantage of the Baron's generosity, and ordered such an assortment of garments that his tailor could hardly bow low enough to express his gratification.

After an excellent lunch in the most expensive restaurant to be found, they walked arm-in-arm westwards along Piccadilly, Mr. Bunker pointing out the various objects of historical or ephemeral interest to be seen in that thoroughfare, the Baron drinking in this information with the serious air of the distinguished traveller.

"And now we come to the Park," said Mr. Bunker. "Guard your heart, Baron."

"Ha, ha, ha!" replied the Baron. "Zo instrogtion is feenished, and now goms entertainment, ha?"

"With the moral always running through it, remember."

"I shall not forget."

The sunshine had brought out a great many carriages and a sprinkling of walkers along the railings. The two friends strolled among them, eyeing the women and stopping now and then to look back at a carriage.

"I suppose," said the Baron, "zat vile you haf been avay your frients have forgot you."

As he spoke a young man looked hard at Mr. Bunker, and even made a movement as though he would stop and speak to him. Mr. Bunker looked blandly through him and walked on.

"Do you not know zat gentleman?"

"Which gentleman?"

"Ze young man zat looked so at you."

"Some young men have a way of staring here, Baron."

A few minutes later a lady in a passing carriage looked round sharply at them with an air of great surprise, and half bowed.

"Surely," exclaimed the Baron, "zat vas a frient of yours!"

"I am not a friend of hers, then," Mr. Bunker replied with a laugh. "Her bow I think must have been aimed at you."

The Baron shook his head, and seemed to be drawing a moral.

"Baron," his friend exclaimed, suddenly, "let us go back; here comes one of our most popular phenomena, a London fog. We need not stay in the Park to observe it."

The sun was already obscured; there stole a most insidious chill through the air; like the changing of a scene on the stage they found themselves in a few minutes walking in a little ring of trees and road and iron railings instead of a wide sunny park; the roar of the streets came from behind a wall of mist that opened mysteriously to let a phantom carriage in and out, and closed silently behind it again.

"I like not zis," said the Baron, with a shiver.

By the time they had found Piccadilly again there was nothing at all to be seen but the light of the nearest lamp as large and far away as a struggling sun, and the shadowy people who flitted by.

Their talk ceased. The Baron turned up his collar and sucked his cigar lugubriously, and Mr. Bunker seemed unusually thoughtful. They had walked nearly as far as Piccadilly Circus when they were pulled up by a cab turning down a side-street. There was a lamp-post at the corner, and under it stood a burly man, his red face quite visible as they came up to his shoulder.

In an instant Mr. Bunker seized the Baron by the arm, pulled him round, and began to walk hastily back again.

"Vat for zis?" said the Baron, in great astonishment.

"We have come too far, thanks to this infernal fog. We must cross the street and take the first turning on the other side. I must apologise, Baron, for my absence of mind."

The cab passed by and the red-faced man strolled on.

"Like lookin' for a needle in a bloomin' haystack," he said to himself. "I might as well go back to Clankwood. 'E's a good riddance, I say."

CHAPTER IV.

The Baron and Mr. Bunker discussed their dinner with the relish of approving connoisseurs. Mr. Bunker commended the hock, and suggested a second bottle; the Baron praised the *entrées,* and insisted on another helping. The frequent laughter arising from their table excited general remark throughout the room, and already the waiters were whispering to the other guests that this was a German nobleman of royal blood engaged in a diplomatic mission of importance, and his friend a ducal member of the English Cabinet, at present, for reasons of state, incognito.

"Bonker!" exclaimed the Baron, "I am in zat frame of head I vant a romance, an adventure" (lowering his voice a little), "mit a beautiful lady, Bonker."

"It must be a romance, Baron?"

"A novel, a story to tell to mine frients. In a strange city man expects strange zings."

"Well, I'll do my best for you, but I confess the provision of romantic adventures is a little outside the programme we've arranged."

"Ha, ha! Ve shall see, ve shall see, Bonker!"

They arrived at the Corinthian Theatre about the middle of the first act, for, as Mr. Bunker explained, it is always well to produce a good first impression, and few more effective means can be devised than working one's way to the middle of a line of stalls with the play already in progress.

Hardly were they seated when the Baron drove his elbow into his friend's ribs (draped for the night, it may be remarked, with one of the Baron's spare dress-coats) and exclaimed in an excited whisper, "Next to you, Bonker! Ach, zehr hüpsch!"

Even before this hint Mr. Bunker had observed that the lady on the other side of him was possessed of exceptional attractions. For a little time he studied her out of the corners of his eyes. He noticed that the stall on the farther side of her was empty, that she once or twice looked round as though she expected somebody, and that she seemed not altogether unconscious of her new neighbours. He further observed that her face was of a type that is more usually engaged in attack than defence.

Then he whispered, "Would you like to know her?"

"Ach, yah!" replied the Baron, eagerly. "Bot—can you?"

Mr. Bunker smiled confidently. A few minutes later he happened to let his programme fall into her lap.

"I beg your pardon," he whispered, softly, and glanced into her eyes with a smile ready.

His usual discernment had not failed him. She smiled, and instantly he produced his.

A little later her opera-glasses happened to slip from her hand, and though they only slipped slowly, it was no doubt owing to his ready presence of mind that their fall was averted.

This time their fingers happened to touch, and they smiled without an apology.

He leant towards her, looking, however, at the play. They shared a laugh over a joke that she might have been excused for not understanding; presently a criticism of some situation escaped him inadvertently, and she smiled again; soon after she gave an exclamation and he answered sympathetically, and at the end of the act the curtain came down on an acquaintance already begun. As the lights were turned up, and here and there men began to go out, she again looked at the entrances in some apparent concern, either lest someone should not come in or lest someone should.

"He is late," said Mr. Bunker, smiling.

She gave a very enticing look of surprise, and consented to smile back before she coyly looked away again.

"An erring husband, I presume."

She admitted that it was in fact a husband who had failed her.

"But," she added, "I'm afraid—I mean I expect he'll come in after the next act. It's so tiresome of him to disappoint me like this."

Mr. Bunker expressed the deepest sympathy with her unfortunate predicament.

"He has his ticket, of course?"

But it seemed that she had both the tickets with her, an arrangement which he immediately denounced as likely to lead to difficulties when her husband arrived. He further, in the most obliging manner, suggested that he should take the ticket for the other seat to the booking office and leave instructions for its being given to the gentleman on his arrival. The lady gave him a curious little glance that seemed to imply a mixture of doubt as to his motives with confidence in his abilities, and then with many thanks agreed to his suggestion. Mr. Bunker took the ticket and rose at once.

"That I may be sure you are in good company while I am away," said he, "permit me to introduce my friend the Baron Rudolph von Blitzenberg."

And the Baron promptly took his vacant seat.

On his return Mr. Bunker found his friend wreathed in smiles and engaged in the most animated conversation with the lady, and before the last act was over, he gathered from such scraps of conversation as reached his ears that Rudolph von Blitzenberg had little to learn in one department of a nobleman's duties.

"I wonder where my husband can be," the lady whispered.

"Ach, heed him not, fair lady," replied the Baron. "Am I not instead of a hosband?"

"I'm afraid you're a very naughty man, Baron."

"Ven I am viz you," the gallant Baron answered, "I forget myself all bot your charms."

These advances being made in the most dulcet tones of which the nobleman was master, and accompanied by the most enamoured expression, it is not surprising that the lady permitted herself to listen to them with perhaps too ready an ear. What Mr. Bunker's arrangement with the booking clerk had been was never quite clear, but certainly the erring husband failed to make his appearance at all, and at the last fall of the curtain she was easily persuaded to let the Baron escort her home.

"I know I ought not, but if a husband deserts one so faithlessly, what can I do?" she said, with a very becoming little shrug of her shoulders and a captivating lift of her eyebrows.

"Ah, vat indeed? He desairves not so fair a consort."

"But won't it be troubling you?"

"Trouble? Pleasure and captivation!"

"Excuse me, Baron," said the voice of Mr. Bunker at his elbow; "if you will wait here at the door I shall send up a cab."

"Goot!" cried the Baron, "a zouzand zanks!"

"I myself," added Mr. Bunker, with a profound bow to the lady, "shall say good night now. The best of luck, Baron!"

In a few minutes a hansom drove up, and the Baron, springing in beside his charge, told the man to drive to 602 Eaton Square.

"Not too qvickly!" he added, in a stage aside.

They reached Trafalgar Square, matters inside going harmoniously as a marriage bell—almost, in fact, too much suggesting that simile.

"Why are we going down Whitehall?" the lady exclaimed, suddenly.

"I know not," replied the Baron, placidly.

"Ask him where he is going!" she said.

The Baron, as in duty bound, asked, and the reassuring reply, "All right, sir," came back through the hole in the roof.

"I seem to know that man's voice," the lady said. "He must have driven me before."

"To me all ze English speak ze same," replied the Baron. "All bot you, my fairest, viz your sound like a—vat you call?—fiddle, is it?"

Though his charmer had serious misgivings regarding their cabman's topographical knowledge, the Baron's company proved so absorbing that it was not till they were being rapidly driven over Vauxhall Bridge that she at last took alarm. At first the Baron strove to soothe her by the most approved Teutonic blandishments, but in time he too began to feel concerned, and in a voice like thunder he repeatedly called upon the driver to stop. No reply was vouchsafed, and the pace merely grew the more reckless.

"Can't you catch the reins?" cried the lady, who had got into a terrible fright.

The Baron twice essayed the feat, but each time a heavy blow over the knuckles from the butt-end of the whip forced him to desist. The lady burst into tears.

The Baron swore in five languages alternately, and still the cab pursued its headlong career through deserted midnight streets, past infrequent policemen and stray belated revellers, on into an unknown wilderness of brick.

"Oh, don't let him murder me!" sobbed the lady.

"Haf cheer, fairest; he shall not vile I am viz you! Gott in himmel, ze rascal! Parbleu und blood! Goddam! Vait till I catch him, hell and blitzen! Haf courage, dear!"

"Oh dear, oh dear!" wailed the lady. "I shall never do it again!"

They must have covered miles, and still the speed never abated, when suddenly, as they were rounding a sharp corner, the horse slipped on the frost-bound road, and in the twinkling of an eye the Baron and the lady were sitting on opposite sides of their fallen steed, and the cabman was rubbing his head some yards in front.

"Teufel!" exclaimed the Baron, rising carefully to his feet. "Ach, mine dearest vun, art thou hurt?"

The lady was silent for a moment, as though trying to decide, and then she burst into hysterical laughter.

"Ach, zo," said the Baron, much relieved, "zen vill I see ze cabman."

That individual was still rubbing his head with a rueful air, and the Baron was about to pour forth all his bottled-up indignation, when at the sight of the driver's face he started back in blank astonishment.

"Bonker!"

"It is I indeed, my dear Baron," replied that gentleman, politely. "I must ask a thousand pardons for causing you this trifling inconvenience. As to your friend, I don't know how I am to make my peace with her."

"Bot—bot vat means zis?" gasped the Baron.

"I was merely endeavouring to provide the spice of romance you required, besides giving you the opportunity of making the lady's better acquaintance. Can I do anything more for you, Baron? And you, my dear lady, can I assist you in any way?"

Both, speaking at once and with some heat, gave a decidedly affirmative answer.

"Where are we?" asked the lady, who hovered between fright and indignation.

Mr. Bunker shrugged his shoulders.

"It would be rash to hazard an opinion," he replied.

"Well!" cried the lady, her indignation quite overcoming her fright. "Do you mean to say you've brought us here against our wills and probably got me into *dreadful* trouble, and you don't even know where we are?"

Mr. Bunker looked up at the heavens with a studious air.

"One *ought* to be able to tell something of our whereabouts from one of those stars," he replied; "but, to tell the truth, I don't quite know which. In short, madame, it is not from want of goodwill, but merely through ignorance, that I cannot direct you."

The lady turned impatiently to the Baron.

"*You've* helped to get me into this mess," she said, tartly. "What do you propose to do?"

"My fairest—"

"Don't!" she interrupted, stamping her foot on the frosty road, and then inconsequently burst into tears. The Baron and Mr. Bunker looked at one another.

"It is a fine night for a walk, and the cab, I'm afraid, is smashed beyond hope of redemption. Give the lady your arm, Baron; we must eventually arrive somewhere."

There was really nothing else for it, so leaving the horse and cab to be recovered by the first policeman who chanced to pass, they set out on foot. At last, after half an hour's ramble through the solitudes of South London, a belated cab was hailed and all three got inside. Once on her way home, the lady's indignation again gave way to fright.

"What *am* I to do? What *am* I to do?" she wailed. "Oh, whatever will my husband say?"

In his most confident and irresistible manner Mr. Bunker told her he would make matters all right for her at whatever cost to himself; and so infectious was his assurance, that, when at last they reached Eaton Square, she allowed him to come up to the door of number 602. The Baron prudently remained in the cab, for, as he explained, "My English, he is unsafe."

After a prolonged knocking and ringing the door at length opened, and an irascible-looking, middle-aged gentleman appeared, arrayed in a dressing-gown.

"Louisa!" he cried. "What the dev—where on earth have you been? The police are looking for you all over London. And may I venture to ask who this is with you?"

Mr. Bunker bowed slightly and raised his hat.

"My dear sir," he said, "we found this lady in a lamentable state of intoxication in the Tottenham Court Road, and as I understand you have a kind of reversionary interest in her, we have brought her here. As for you, sir, your appearance is so unprepossessing that I am unable to remain any longer. Good night," and raising his hat again he entered the cab and drove off, assuring the Baron that matters were satisfactorily arranged.

"So you have had your adventure, Baron," he added, with a smile.

For a minute or two the Baron was silent. Then he broke into a cheerful guffaw, "Ha, ha, ha! You are a fonny devil, Bonker! Ach, bot it vas pleasant vile it lasted!"

CHAPTER V.

A few days passed in the most entertaining manner. A menu of amusements was regularly prepared suitable to a catholic taste, and at every turn the Baron was struck by the enterprise and originality of his friend. He had, however, a national bent for serious inquiry, and now and then doubts crossed his mind whether with all his moral drawing, he was acquiring quite as much solid information as he had set out to gain. This idea grew upon him, till one morning, after gazing for some time at the English newspaper he always made a point of reading, he suddenly exclaimed, "Bonker, I haf a doubt!"

"I have many," replied Mr. Bunker; "in fact, I have few positive ideas left."

"Bot mine is a particulair doubt. Do I lairn enoff?"

"My own conception of enough learning, Baron, is a thing like a threepenny-bit—the smallest coin one can do one's marketing with."

"And yet," said the Baron, solemnly, "for my own share, I am not satisfied. I vould lairn more of ze British institutions; so far I haf lairned of ze pleasures only."

"My dear Baron, they are the British institutions."

The Baron shook his head and fell to his paper again, while Mr. Bunker stretched himself on the sofa and gazed through his cigar-smoke at the ceiling. Suddenly the Baron gave an exclamation of horror.

"My dear Baron, what is the matter?"

"Yet anozer outrage!" cried the Baron. "Zese anarchists, zey are too scandalous. At all ze stations zere are detectives, and all ze ships are being vatched. Ach, it is terrible!"

Mr. Bunker seemed struck with an idea, for he stared at the ceiling without making any reply, and his eyes, had the Baron seen them, twinkled curiously.

At last the Baron laid down his paper.

"Vell, vat shall ve do?" he asked.

"Let us come first to Liverpool Street Station, if you don't mind, Baron," his friend suggested. "I have something in the cloak-room there I want to pick up."

"My dear Bonker, I shall go vere you vill; bot remember I vant today more instrogtion and less entertainment."

"You wish to see the practical side of English life?"

"Yah—zat is, yes."

Mr. Bunker smiled.

"Then I must entertain myself."

As they drove down he was in his wittiest humour, and the Baron, in spite of his desire for instruction, was more charmed with his friend than ever.

"Vat fonny zing vill you do next, eh?" he asked, as they walked arm-in-arm into the station.

"I am no more the humourist, my dear Baron—I shall endeavour to edify you."

They had arrived at a busy hour, when the platforms were crowded with passengers and luggage. A train had just come in, and around it the bustle was at its height, and the confusion most bewildering.

"Wait for me here," said Mr. Bunker; "I shall be back in a minute."

He started in the direction of the cloak-room, and then, doubling back through the crowd, walked down the platform and stopped opposite a luggage-van. An old gentleman, beside himself with irritation, was struggling with the aid of a porter to collect his luggage, and presently he left the pile he had got together and made a rush in the direction of a large portmanteau that was just being tumbled out. Instantly Mr. Bunker picked up a handbag from the heap and walked quickly off with it.

"Here you are, Baron," he said, as he came up to his friend. "I find there is something else I must do, so do you mind holding this bag for a few minutes? If you will walk up and down in front of the refreshment-rooms here, I'll find you more easily. Is it troubling you too much?"

"Not vun bit, Bonker. I am in your sairvice."

He put the bag into the Baron's hand with his pleasantest smile, and turned away. Rounding a corner, he came cautiously back again through the crowd and stepped up to a policeman.

"Keep your eye on that man, officer," he said, in a low confidential voice, and an air of quiet authority, "and put your plain-clothes men on his track. I know him for one of the most dangerous anarchists."

The man started and stared hard at the Baron, and presently that unconscious nobleman, pacing the platform in growing wonder at Mr. Bunker's lengthy absence, and looking anxiously round him on all sides, noticed with surprise that a number of quietly dressed men, with no apparent business in the station, were eyeing him with, it seemed to him, an interest that approached suspicion. In time he grew annoyed, he returned their glances with his haughtiest and most indignant look, and finally, stepping up to one of them, asked in no friendly voice, "Vat for do you vatch me?"

The man returned an evasive answer, and passing one of his fellow-officers, whispered, "Foreign; I was sure of it."

At last the Baron could stand it no longer, and laying the bag down by the door of the refreshment-room, turned hastily away. On the instant Mr. Bunker, who had watched these proceedings from a safe distance, cried in a loud and agonised voice, "Down with your men, sergeant! Down, lie down! It will explode in twenty seconds!"

And as he spoke he threw himself flat on his face. So infectious were his commanding voice and his note of alarm that one after another, detectives, passengers, and porters, cast themselves at full length on the platform. The Baron, filled with terror of anarchist plots, was one of the first to prostrate himself, and at that there could be no further doubt of the imminence of the peril.

The cabs rattled and voices sounded from outside; an engine whistled and shunted at a far platform, but never before at that hour of the day had Liverpool Street Station been so silent. All held their breath and heard their hearts thump as they gazed in horrible fascination at that fatal bag, or with closed eyes stumbled through a hasty prayer. Fully a minute passed, and the suspense was growing intolerable, when with a loud oath an old gentleman rose to his feet and walked briskly up to the bag.

"Have a care, sir! For Heaven's sake have a care!" cried Mr. Bunker; but the old gentleman merely bent over the terrible object, and, picking it up, exclaimed in bewildered wrath, "It's my bag! Who the devil brought it here, and what's the meaning of this d—d nonsense?"

"Ha, ha, ha, ha, ha!" roared Mr. Bunker; while like sheepish mushrooms the people sprang up on all sides.

"My dear sir," said Mr. Bunker, coming up to the old gentleman, and raising his hat with his most affable air, "permit me to congratulate you on recovering your lost property, and allow me further to introduce my friend the Baron Rudolph von Blitzenberg."

"Baron von damned-humbug!" cried the old gentleman. "Did you take my bag, sir? And if so, are you a thief or a lunatic?"

For an instant even Mr. Bunker himself seemed a trifle taken aback; then he replied politely, "I am not a thief, sir."

"Then what *'ave* you been doing?" demanded the sergeant.

"Merely demonstrating to my friend the Baron the extraordinary vigilance of the English police."

For a time neither the old gentleman nor the sergeant seemed quite capable of taking the same view of the episode as Mr. Bunker, and, curiously enough, the Baron seemed not disinclined to let his friend extricate himself as best he could. No one, however, could resist Mr. Bunker, and before very long he and the Baron were driving up Bishopsgate Street together, with the old gentleman's four-wheeler lumbering in front of them.

"Well, Baron, are you satisfied with your morning's instruction?" asked his friend.

"A German nobleman is not used to be in soch a position," replied the Baron, stiffly.

"You must admit, however, that the object-lesson in the detection of anarchy was neatly presented."

"I admit nozing of ze kind," said the Baron, stolidly.

For the rest of the drive he sat obdurately silent. He went to his room with the mien of an offended man. During lunch he only opened his lips to eat.

On his side Mr. Bunker maintained a cheerful composure, and seemed not a whit put about by his friend's lack of appreciation.

"Anozzer bottle of claret," said the Baron, gruffly, to a waiter.

Mr. Bunker let him consume it entirely by himself, awaiting the results with patience. Gradually his face relaxed a little, until all at once, when the bump in the bottom of the bottle was beginning to appear above the wine, the whole room was startled by a stentorian, "Ha, ha, ha!"

"My dear Bonker!" cried the Baron, when he had finished laughing, "forgif me! I begin for to see ze moral, ha, ha, ha!"

CHAPTER VI.

The Baron expressed no further wish for instruction, but, instead, he began to show a desire for society.

"Doesn't one fool suffice?" his friend asked.

"Ach, yes, my vise fool; ha, ha, ha! Bot sometimes I haf ze craving for peoples, museec, dancing—in vun vord, society, Bonker!"

"But this is not the season, Baron. You wouldn't mix with any but the best society, would you?"

"Zere are some nobles in town. In my paper I see Lord zis, Duke of zat, in London. Pairhaps my introdogtions might be here now."

This suggestion seemed to strike Mr. Bunker unfavourably.

"My company is beginning to pall, is it, Baron?"

"Ach, no, dear Bonker! I vould merely go out jost vunce or tvice. Haf you no friends now in town?"

An idea seemed to seize Mr. Bunker.

"Let me see the paper," he said.

After perusing it carefully for a little, he at last exclaimed in a tone of pleased discovery, "Hullo! I see that Lady Tulliwuddle is giving a reception and dance tonight. Most of the smart people in town just now are sure to be there. Would you care to go, Baron?"

"Ach, surely," said the Baron, eagerly. "Bot haf you been invited, Bonker?"

"Oh, I used to have a standing invitation to Lady Tulliwuddle's dances, and I'm certain she would be glad to see me again."

"Can you take me?"

"Of course, my dear Baron, she will be honoured."

"Goot!" cried the Baron. "Ve shall go."

Mr. Bunker explained that it was the proper thing to arrive very late, and so it was not until after twelve o'clock that they left the Hôtel Mayonaise for the regions of Belgravia. The Baron, primed with a bottle of champagne, and arrayed in a costume which Mr. Bunker had assured him was the very latest extreme of fashion, and which included a scarlet watered-silk waistcoat, a pair of white silk socks, and a lavender tie, was in a condition of cheerfulness verging closely on hilarity. Mr. Bunker, that, as he said, he might better serve as a foil to his friend's splendour, went more inconspicuously dressed, but was likewise well charged with champagne. He too was in his happiest vein, and the vision of the Baron's finery appeared to afford him peculiar gratification.

Their hansom stopped in front of a large and gaily lit-up mansion, with an awning leading to the door, and a cluster of carriages and footmen by the kerbstone. They entered, and having divested themselves of their coats, Mr. Bunker proposed that they should immediately seek the supper-room.

"Bot should I not be first introduced to mine hostess?" asked the Baron.

"My dear Baron! A formal reception of the guests is entirely foreign to English etiquette."

"Zo? I did not know zat."

The supper-room was crowded, and having secured a table with some difficulty, Mr. Bunker entered immediately into conversation with a solitary young gentleman who was consuming a plate of oysters. Before they had exchanged six sentences the young man had entirely succumbed to Mr. Bunker's address, aided possibly by the young man's supper.

"Permit me to introduce my friend the Baron Rudolph von

Blitzenberg, a nobleman strange as yet to England, but renowned throughout his native land alike for his talents and his lofty position," said Mr. Bunker.

"Ach, my good friend," exclaimed the Baron, grasping the young man's hand, "das ist Bonker's vat you call nonsense; bot I am delighted, zehr delighted, to meet you, and if you gom to Bavaria you most shoot vid me! Bravo! Ha!"

From which it may be gathered that the Baron was in a genial humour.

"Who is that girl?" asked Mr. Bunker, pointing to an extremely pretty damsel just leaving the room.

"Oh, that's my cousin, Lady Muriel Hilton. She's thought rather pretty, I believe," answered the young man.

"Do you mind introducing me?"

"Certainly," said their new friend. "Come along."

As they were passing through the room a little incident occurred that, if the Baron's perceptions had been keener, might have given him cause for some speculation. Two men standing by the door looked hard at Mr. Bunker, and then at each other, and as the Baron passed them he heard one say, "It looks devilish like him."

"He has shaved, then," said the other.

"Evidently," replied the first speaker; "but I thought he was unlikely to appear in any society for some time."

They both laughed, and the Baron heard no more.

When they reached the ballroom the band was striking up a polka, and presently Mr. Bunker, with his accustomed grace, was tearing round the room with Lady Muriel, while the Baron—the delight of all eyes in his red waistcoat—led out her sister. In a very short time the other dancers found the Baron and his friend's onslaught so vigorous that prudence compelled them to take shelter along the wall, and from a safe distance admire the evolutions of these two mysterious guests.

Mr. Bunker was enlivening the monotony of the polka by the judicious introduction of hornpipe steps, while the Baron, his coat-tails high above his head, shouted and stamped in his wild career.

"Do stop for a minute, Baron," gasped his fair partner.

"Himmel, nein!" roared the Baron. "I haf gom here for to dance! Ha, Bonker, ha!"

At last Lady Muriel had to stop through sheer exhaustion, but Mr. Bunker, merely letting her go, pursued his solitary way, double-shuffling and kicking unimpeded.

The Baron stopped, breathless, to admire him. Round and round he went, the only figure in the middle of the room, his arms akimbo, his feet rat-tatting and kicking to the music, while high above the band resounded his friend's shouts of "Bravo, Bonker! Wunderschön! Gott in himmel, higher, higher!" till at length, missing the wall in an attempt to find support, the Baron dropped with a thud into a sitting posture and continued his demonstrations from the floor.

Meanwhile their alarmed hostess was holding a hasty consultation with her husband, and when the music at last stopped and Mr. Bunker was advancing with his most courteous air towards his late partner, Lord Tulliwuddle stepped up to him and touched his arm.

"May I speak to you, sir?" he said.

"Certainly," replied Mr. Bunker. "I shall be honoured. Excuse me for one moment, Lady Muriel."

"At whose invitation have you come here tonight?" demanded his host, sternly.

"I have the pleasure of addressing Lord Tulliwuddle, have I not?"

"You have, sir."

Mr. Bunker bent towards him and whispered something in his ear.

"From Scotland Yard?" exclaimed his lordship.

"Hush!" said Mr. Bunker, glancing cautiously round the room, and then he added, with an air of impressive gravity, "You have a bathroom on the third floor, I believe?"

"I have," replied his host in great surprise.

"Has it a bell?"

"No, I believe not."

"Ah, I thought so. If you will favour me by coming upstairs for a minute, my Lord, you will avoid a serious private scandal. Say nothing about it at present to anyone."

In blank astonishment and some alarm Lord Tulliwuddle went up with him to the third floor, where the house was still and the sounds of revelry reached faintly.

"What does this mean, sir?" he asked.

"If I am right in my conjectures you will need no explanation from me, my Lord."

His lordship opened a door, and turning on an electric light, revealed a small and ordinary-looking bathroom.

"Ha, no bell—excellent!" said Mr. Bunker.

"What are you doing with the key?" exclaimed his host.

"Good night, my Lord. I shall tell them to send up breakfast at nine," said Mr. Bunker, and stepping quickly out, he shut and locked the door.

A minute later he was back in the ballroom looking anxiously for the Baron, but that nobleman was nowhere to be seen.

"The devil!" he said to himself. "Can they have tackled him too?"

But as he ran downstairs a gust of cheerful laughter set his mind at ease.

"Ha, ha, ha! Vere is old Bonker? He also vill shoot vid me!"

"Here I am, my dear Baron," he exclaimed gaily, as he tracked the voice into the supper-room.

"Ach, mine dear Bonker!" cried the Baron, folding him in his muscular embrace, "I haf here met friends, ve are merry! Ve drink to Bavaria, to England, to everyzing!"

The "friends" consisted of two highly amused young men and two half-scandalised, half-hysterical ladies, into the midst of whose supper-table the Baron had projected himself with infectious hilarity. They all looked up with great curiosity at Mr. Bunker, but that gentleman was not in the least put about. He bowed politely to the table generally, and took his friend by the arm.

"It is time we were going, Baron, I'm afraid," he said.

"Vat for? Ah, not yet, Bonker, not yet. I am enjoying myself down to ze floor. I most dance again, Bonker, jost vunce more," pleaded the Baron.

"My dear Baron, the noblemen of highest rank must always leave first, and people are talking of going now. Come along, old man."

"Ha, is zat so?" said the Baron. "Zen vill I go. Good night!" he cried, waving his hand to the room generally. "Ven you gom to Bavaria you most all shoot vid me. Bravo, my goot Bonker! Ha! ha!"

As they turned away from the table, one of the young men, who had been looking very hard at Mr. Bunker, rose and touched his sleeve.

"I say, aren't you—?" he began.

"Possibly I am," interrupted Mr. Bunker, "only I haven't the slightest recollection of the fact."

An astonished lady was indicated by Mr. Bunker as the hostess, and to her the Baron bade an affectionate adieu. He handed a sovereign to the footman, embraced the butler, and as they sped eastwards in their hansom, a rousing chorus from the two friends awoke the echoes of Piccadilly.

"Bravo, Bonker! Himmel, I haf enjoyed myself!" sighed the exhausted Baron.

CHAPTER VII.

The Baron and Mr. Bunker discussed a twelve o'clock breakfast with the relish of men who had done a good night's work. The Baron was full of his exploits. "Ze lofly Lady Hilton" and his new "friends" seemed to have made a vivid impression.

"Zey vill be in ze Park today, of course?" he suggested.

"Possibly," replied Mr. Bunker, without any great enthusiasm.

"But surely."

"After a dance it is rather unlikely."

"Ze Lady Hilton did say she vent to ze Park."

"Today, Baron?"

"I do not remember today. I did dance so hard I was not perhaps distinct. But I shall go and see."

As Mr. Bunker's attempts to throw cold water on this scheme proved quite futile, he made a graceful virtue of necessity, dressed himself with care, and set out in the afternoon for the Park. They had only walked as far as Piccadilly Circus when in the crowd at the corner his eye fell upon a familiar figure. It was the burly, red-faced man.

"The devil! Moggridge again!" he muttered.

For a moment he thought they were going to pass unobserved: then the man turned his head their way, and Mr. Bunker saw him start. He never looked over his shoulder, but after walking a little farther he called the Baron's attention to a shop window, and they stopped to look at it. Out of the corner of his eye he saw Moggridge about twenty yards behind them stopping too. He was glancing towards them very doubtfully. Evidently his mind was not yet made up, and at once Mr. Bunker's fertile brain began to revolve plans.

A little farther on they paused before another window, and exactly the same thing happened. Then Mr. Bunker made up his mind. He looked carefully at the cabs, and at last observed a smart-looking young man driving a fresh likely horse at a walking pace beside the pavement.

He caught the driver's eye and raised his stick, and turning suddenly to the Baron with a gesture of annoyance, exclaimed, "Forgive my rudeness, Baron, I'm afraid I must leave you. I had clean forgotten an important engagement in the city for this afternoon."

"Appointment in ze city?" said the Baron in considerable surprise. "I did not know you had friends in ze city."

"I have just heard from my father's man of business, and I'm afraid it would be impolitic not to see him. Do you mind if I leave you here?"

"Surely, my dear fellow, I vould not stop you. Already I feel at home by myself."

"Then we shall meet at the hotel before dinner. Good luck with the ladies, Baron."

Mr. Bunker jumped into the cab, saying only to the driver, "To the city, as quick as you can."

"What part, sir?"

"Oh, say the Bank. Hurry up!"

Then as the man whipped up, Mr. Bunker had a glimpse of Moggridge hailing another cab, and peeping cautiously through the little window at the back he saw him starting in hot pursuit. He took five shillings out of his pocket and opened the trap-door in the roof.

"Do you see that other cab chasing us, with a red-faced man inside?"

"Yes, sir."

Mr. Bunker handed his driver the money.

"Get rid of him, then. Take me anywhere through the city you like, and when he's off the scent let me know."

"Very good, sir," replied the driver, cracking his whip till his steed began to move past the buses and the other cabs like a train.

On they flew, clatter and jingle, twisting like a snipe through the traffic. Mr. Bunker perceived that he had a good horse and a good driver, and he smiled in pleasant excitement. He lit a cigar, leaned his arms on the doors, and settled himself to enjoy the race.

The black lions of Trafalgar Square flew by, then the colossal hotels of Northumberland Avenue and the railway bridge at Charing Cross, and they were going at a gallop along the Embankment. He got swift glimpses of other cabs and foot-passengers, the trees seemed to flit past like telegraph-posts on a railway, the barges and lighters on the river dropped one by one behind them: it was a fair course for a race, with never a check before Blackfriar's Bridge.

As they turned into Queen Victoria Street he opened the lid and asked, "Are they still in sight?"

"Yes, sir; I'm afraid we ain't gaining much yet. But I'll do it, sir, no fears."

Mr. Bunker lay back and laughed.

"This is better than the Park," he said to himself.

They had a fine drive up Queen Victoria Street before they plunged into the whirlpool of traffic at the Bank. They were slowly making their way across when the driver, spying an opening in another stream, abruptly wheeled round for Cornhill, and presently they were off again at top speed.

"Thrown them off?" asked Mr. Bunker.

"Tried to, sir, but they were too sharp and got clear away too."

Mr. Bunker saw that it was going to be a stern chase, and laughed again. In order that he might not show ostensibly that he was running away, he resisted the temptation of having another peep through the back, and resigned himself to the chances of the chase.

Through and through the lanes and byways of the city they drove, and after each double the answer from the box was always the same. The cab behind could not be shaken off.

"Work your way round to Holborn and try a run west," Mr. Bunker suggested.

So after a little they struck Newgate Street, and presently their steed stretched himself again in Holborn Viaduct.

"Gaining now, cabby?"

"A little, sir, I think."

Mr. Bunker sat placidly till they were well along Holborn before he inquired again.

"Can't get rid of 'im no 'ow. Afride it ain't much good, sir."

Mr. Bunker passed up five shillings more.

"Keep your tail up. You'll do it yet," he exhorted. "Try a turn north; you may bother him among the squares."

So they doubled north, and as the evening closed in their wearied horse was lashed through a maze of monotonous streets and tarnished Bloomsbury Squares. And still the other cab stuck to their trail. But when they emerged on the Euston Road, Mr. Bunker was as cheerful as ever.

"They can't last much longer," he said to his driver. "Turn up Regent's Park way."

A little later he put the usual question and got the same unvarying answer.

The horse was evidently beginning to fail, and he saw that this chariot-race must soon come to an end. The street-lamps and the shop windows were all lit up by this time, and the dusk was pretty thick. It seemed to him that he might venture to try his luck on foot, and he began to look out for an opening where a cab could not follow.

They were flogging along a noisy stone-paved road where there was little other traffic; on one side stood an unbroken row of houses, and on the other were small semi-detached villas with little strips of garden about them. All at once he saw a doctor's red lamp over the door of one of these half villas, and an inspiration came upon him.

"One can always visit a doctor," he said to himself, and smiled in great amusement at something in the reflection.

He stopped the cab, handed the man half a sovereign, and saying only, "Drive away again, quickly," jumped out, glanced at the name on the plate, and pulled the bell. As he waited on the step he saw the other cab stop a little way back, and his pursuer emerge.

A frowsy little servant opened the door.

"Is Dr. Twiddel at home?" he asked.

"Dr. Twiddel's abroad, sir," said the maid.

"No one in at all, then?"

"Dr. Billson sees 'is patients, sir—w'en there his any."

"When do you expect Dr. Billson?"

"In about an hour, sir, 'e usually comes hin."

"Excellent!" thought Mr. Bunker. Aloud he said, "Well, I'm a patient. I'll come in and wait."

He stepped in, and the door banged behind him.

CHAPTER VIII.

"This w'y, sir," said the maid, and Mr. Bunker found himself in the little room where this story opened.

The moment he was alone he went to the window and peeped cautiously between the slats of the venetian blind.

The street was quiet, both cabs had disappeared, and for a minute or two he could see nothing even of Moggridge. Then a figure moved carefully from the shelter of a bush a little way down the railings, and, after a quick look at the house, stepped back again.

"He means to play the waiting game," said Mr. Bunker to himself. "Long may you wait, my wary Moggridge!"

He took a rapid survey of the room. He saw the medical library, the rented furniture, and the unlit gas-stove; and at last his eye fell upon a box of cigarettes. To one of these he helped himself and leaned his back against the mantelpiece.

"There must be at least one room at the back," he reflected; "that room must have a window, and beyond that window there is all London to turn to. Friend Moggridge, I trust you are prepared to spend the evening behind your bush."

He had another look through the blind and shook his head.

"A little too light yet—I'd better wait for a quarter of an hour or so."

To while away the time he proceeded to make a tour of the room, for, as he said to himself, when in an unknown country any information may possibly come in useful. There was nothing whatever from which he could draw even the most superficial deduction till he came to the writing-desk. Here a heap of bills were transfixed by a long skewer, and at his first glance at the uppermost his face assumed an expression of almost ludicrous bewilderment. He actually rubbed his eyes before he looked a second time.

"One dozen shirts," he read, "four under-flannels, four pair socks, one dozen handkerchiefs, two sleeping-suits—marked Francis Beveridge! The account rendered to Dr. G. Twiddel! What in the name of wonderment is the meaning of this?"

He sat down with the bill in his hand and gazed hard at it.

"Precisely my outfit," he said to himself.

"Am I—Does it? What a rum thing!"

He sat for about ten minutes looking hard at the door. Then he burst out laughing, resumed in a moment his air of philosophical opportunism, and set about a further search of the desk. He looked at the bills and seemed to find nothing more to interest him. Then he glanced at one or two letters in the drawers, threw the first few back again, and at last paused over one.

"Twiddel to Billson," he said to himself. "This may possibly be worth looking at."

It was dated more than a month back from the town of Fogelschloss.

"Dear Tom," it ran, "we are having an A-1 time. Old Welsh is in splendid form, doing the part to perfection. He has never given himself away yet, not even when drunk, which, I am sorry to say, he has been too often. But then old Welsh is so funny when he is drunk that it makes him all the more like the original, or at least what the original is supposed to be.

"Of course we don't dare to venture into places where we would see too many English. This is quite an amusing place for a German town, some baths and a kind of a gambling-table, and some pretty girls—for Germans. There is a sporting aristocrat here, in an old castle, who is very friendly, and is much impressed with Welsh's account of his family plate and deer-forest, and has asked us once or twice to come out and see him. We are no end of swells, I assure you.

"Ta, ta, old chap. Hope the practice prospers in your hands. Don't kill *all* the patients before I come back.—Ever thine,

"GEORGE TWIDDEL."

"From this I conclude that Dr. Twiddel is on the festive side of forty," he reflected; "there are elements of mystery and a general atmosphere of alcohol about it, but that's all, I'm afraid."

He put it back in the drawer, but the bill he slipped into his pocket.

"And now," thought he, "it is time I made the first move."

After waiting for a minute or two to make sure that everything was quiet, he gently stepped out into a little linoleum-carpeted hall. On the right hand was the front door, on the left two others that must, he thought, open into rooms on the back. He chose the nearer at a venture, and entered boldly. It was quite dark. He closed the door again softly, struck a match, and looked round the room. It seemed to be Dr. Twiddel's dining- and sitting-room.

"Pipes, photographs, well-sat-in chairs," he observed, "and a window."

He pulled aside the blind and looked out into the darkness of a strip of back-garden. For a minute he listened intently, but no sound came from the house. Then he threw up the sash and scrambled out. It was quite dark by this time: he was enclosed between two rows of vague, black houses, with bright windows here and there, and chimney-cans faintly cutting their uncouth designs among a few pale London stars. The space between was filled with the two lines of little gardens and the ranks of walls, and in the middle the black chasm of a railway cutting.

A frightened cat bolted before him as he hurried down to the foot of the strip, but that was all the life he saw. He looked over the wall right into the deep crevasse. A little way off, on the one hand, hung a cluster of signal-lights, and the shining rails reflected them all along to the mouth of a tunnel on the other. Turning his head this way and that, there was nothing to be seen anywhere else but garden wall after garden wall.

"It's a choice between a hurdle-race through these gardens, a cat-walk along this wall, and a descent into the cutting," he reflected. "The walls look devilish high and the cutting devilish deep. Hang me if I know which road to take."

While he was still debating this somewhat perplexing question, he felt the ground begin to quiver under him. Through the hum of London there gradually arose a louder roar, and in a minute the head-lights of an engine flashed out of the tunnel. One after another a string of bright carriages followed it, each more slowly than the carriage in front, till the whole train was at a standstill below him with the red signal-lamp against it.

In an instant his decision was taken. At the peril of life and garments he scrambled down the rocky bank, picking as he went an empty first-class compartment, and just as the train began to move again he swung himself up and sprang into a carriage.

Unfortunately he had chosen the wrong one in his haste, and as he opened the door he saw a comical vision of a stout little old gentleman huddling into the farther corner in the most dire consternation.

"Who are you, sir? What do you want, sir?" spluttered the old gentleman. "If you come any nearer me, sir—one step, sir!—I shall instantly communicate with the guard! I have no money about me. Go away, sir!"

"I regret to learn that you have no money," replied Mr. Bunker, imperturbably; "but I am sorry that I am not at present in a condition to offer a loan."

He sat down and smiled amicably, but the little gentleman was not to be quieted so easily. Seeing that no violence was apparently intended, his fright changed into respectable indignation.

"You needn't try to be funny with me, sir. You are committing an illegal act. You have placed yourself in an uncommonly serious position, sir."

"Indeed, sir?" replied Mr. Bunker. "I myself should have imagined that by remaining on the rails I should have been much more seriously situated."

The old gentleman looked at him like an angry small dog that longs to bite if it only dared.

"What is the meaning of this illegal intrusion?" he demanded. "Who are you? Where did you come from?"

"I had the misfortune, sir," explained Mr. Bunker, politely, "to drop my hat out of the window of a neighbouring carriage. While I was picking it up the train started, and I had to enter the first compartment I could find. I am sorry that my entry frightened you."

"Frightened me!" spluttered the old gentleman. "I am not afraid, sir. I am an honest man who need fear no one, sir. I do not believe you dropped your hat. It is perfectly uninjured."

"It may be news to you, sir," replied Mr. Bunker, "that by gently yet firmly passing the sleeve of your coat round your hat in the direction of the nap, it is possible to restore the gloss. Thus," and suiting the action to the word he took off his hat, drew his coat-sleeve across it, and with a genial smile at the old gentleman, replaced it on his head.

But his neighbour was evidently of that truculent disposition which merely growls at blandishments. He snorted and replied testily, "That is all very well, sir, but I don't believe a word of it."

"If you prefer it, then, I fell off the telegraph wires in an attempt to recover my boots."

The old gentleman became purple in the face.

"Have a care, sir! I am a director of this company, and at the next station I shall see that you give a proper account of yourself. And here we are, sir. I trust you have a more credible story in readiness."

As he spoke they drew up beside an underground platform, and the irascible old gentleman, with a very threatening face that was not yet quite cleared of alarm, bustled out in a prodigious hurry. Mr.

Bunker lay back in his seat and replied with a smile, "I shall be delighted to tell any story within the bounds of strict propriety."

But the moment he saw the irate director disappear in the crowd he whipped out too, and with the least possible delay transferred himself into a third-class carriage.

From his seat near the window he watched the old gentleman hurry back with three officials at his heels, and hastily search each first-class compartment in turn. The last one was so near him that he could hear his friend say, "Damn it, the rascal has bolted in the crowd!"

And with that the four of them rushed off to the barrier to intercept or pursue this suspicious character. Then the whistle blew, and as the train moved off Mr. Bunker remarked complacently, if a little mysteriously, to himself, "Well, whoever I am, it would seem I'm rather difficult to catch."

CHAPTER IX.

Mr. Bunker arrived at the Hôtel Mayonaise in what, from his appearance, was an unusually reflective state of mind for him. The other visitors, many of whom had begun to regard him and his noble friend with great interest, saw him pass through the crowd in the hall and about the lifts with a thoughtful air. He went straight to the Baron's room. Outside the door he paused for an instant to set his face in a cheerful smile, and then burst gaily in upon his friend.

"Well, my dear Baron!" he cried, "what luck in the Park?"

The Baron was pulling his moustache over an English novel. He laid down his book and frowned at Mr. Bunker.

"I do not onderstand your English vays," he replied.

Mr. Bunker perceived that something was very much amiss, nor was he without a suspicion of the cause. He laughed, however, and asked, "What's the matter, old man?"

"I vent to ze Park," said the Baron, with a solemn deliberation that evidently came hardly to him. "I entered ze Park. I vas dressed, as you know, viz taste and appropriety. I vas sober, as you know. I valked under ze trees, and I looked agreeably at ze people. Goddam!"

"My dear Baron!" expostulated Mr. Bunker.

The Baron resumed his intense composure with a great effort.

"Not long vas ven I see ze Lady Hilton drive past mit ze ozzer

Lady Hilton and vun old lady. I raise my hat—no bow from zem. 'Pairhaps,' I zink, 'zey see me not.' Zey stop by ze side to speak viz a gentleman. I gomed up and again I raise my hat and I say, 'How do you do, Lady Hilton? I hope you are regovered from ze dance.' Zat was gorrect, vas it not?"

"Perfectly," replied Mr. Bunker, with great gravity.

"Zen vy did ze Lady Hilton schream and ze ozzer Lady Hilton cry, 'Ach, zat German man!' And vy did ze old lady schream to ze gentleman, 'Send him avay! How dare you? Insolence!' and such-like vords?"

"What remarkable conduct, my dear Baron!" said Mr. Bunker.

"Remargable!" roared the justly incensed Baron. "Is it not more zan *remargable*? Donner und blitzen! Mon Dieu! Blood! I know not ze English vord so bad enoff for soch conduct."

"It must have been a joke," his friend suggested, soothingly.

"Vun dashed bad joke, zen! Ze gentleman said to me, 'Get out of zis, you rasgal!' 'Vat mean you, sare?' say I. 'You know quite vell,' said he. 'Glear out!'

So I gave him my card and tell him I would be glad to see his frient zat he should send, for zat I vas not used to be called zo. Zen I raise my hat to ze Lady Hilton and say, 'Adieu, madame, I know now ze English lady,' and I valk on. Himmel!"

"What a very extraordinary affair, Baron!"

The Baron grunted with inarticulate indignation and nearly pulled his moustache out by the roots. Abruptly he broke out again, "English ladies? I do not believe zey are ladies! Never haf I been treated zo! Vat do you mean, Bonker, by taking me among soch peoples?"

"*I,* my dear Baron? It was not I who introduced you to the Hiltons. I never saw them before."

The difficulty of attaching any blame to his friend seemed to have anything but a soothing effect on the Baron. You could almost fancy that you heard his tail lash the floor.

"Zat vas not all," he continued, after a short struggle with his wrath. "I valked on, and soon I see two of ze frients I made last night at supper."

"Which two?"

"Ze yong man zat spoke to you ven you rise from ze table, and vun of ze ladies. Again I raise my hat and say, 'How do you do? I hope zat you are regovered from ze dance.' Zat is gorrect, you say?"

"Under most circumstances."

"Ze man stared at me, and ze voman—I vill not say lady—says to him zo zat I can hear, 'Zat awful German!' Ze man says, 'Zo it is,' and laughed. 'I haf ze pleasure of meeting you last night at ze Lady Tollyvoddle,' I said. 'I remember,' he said; 'but I haf no vish to meet you again.' I take out my card to gif him, but he only said, 'Go avay, or I vill call ze police!' 'Ze police! To me, Baron von Blitzenberg! Teufel!' I replied."

"And that was all, Baron?" asked Mr. Bunker, in what seemed rather like a tone of relief.

"No; suddenly he did turn back and said, 'By ze vay, who vas zat viz you last night?' To vich I replied, 'If you address me again, my man, I vill call ze police. Go avay!'"

"Bravo, Baron! Ha, ha, ha! Excellent!" laughed Mr. Bunker.

This applause served to reinstate the Baron a little in his own good opinion. He laughed too, though rather noisily than heartily, and suddenly became grave again.

"Vat means zis, Bonker? Vat haf I done? Vy should zey treat me zo?"

"Well, you see, my dear Baron," his friend explained, "I ought to have warned you that it is not usual in England to address ladies you have met at a dance without some direct invitation on their part. At the same time, it is evident that the Hiltons and the other man, who of course must be connected with the Foreign Office, are aware of some sudden strain in the diplomatic relations between England and Germany, which as yet is unknown to the public. Your ancient name and your high rank have naturally led them to conclude that you are an agent of the German Government, and an international significance was of course attached to your presence in the Park. I certainly think they took a most outrageous advantage of a trifling detail of etiquette to repulse you; but then you must remember, Baron, that their families might have been seriously compromised with the Government if they had been seen with so prominent a member of the German aristocracy in the middle of Hyde Park."

"Zo?" said the Baron, thoughtfully. "I begin to onderstand. My name, as you say, is cairtainly distinguished. Bot zen should I remain in London?"

"Just what I was wondering, Baron. What do you say to a trip down to St Egbert's-on-Sea? It's a very select watering-place, and we might spend a week or two there very pleasantly."

"Egxellent!" said the Baron; "ven shall we start?"

"Tomorrow morning."

"Goot! Zo let it be. I am tired of London and of ze English ladies' manners. Police to ze Baron von Blitzenberg! Ve shall go to St Egbert's, Bonker!"

PART III.

CHAPTER I.

The Baron and Mr. Bunker walked arm-in-arm along the esplanade at St Egbert's-on-Sea.

"Aha!" said the Baron, "zis is more fresh zan London!"

"Yes," replied his friend; "we are now in the presence of that stimulating element which provides patriotic Britons with music-hall songs, and dyspeptic Britons with an appetite."

A stirring breeze swept down the long white esplanade, threatening hats and troubling skirts; the pale-green south-coast sea rumbled up the shingle; the day was bright and pleasant for the time of year, and drove the Baron's mischances from his head; altogether it seemed to Mr. Bunker that the omens were good. They were both dressed in the smartest of tweed suits, and walked jauntily, like men who knew their own value. Every now and then, as they passed a pretty face, the Baron would say, "Aha, Bonker! Zat is not so bad, eh?"

And Mr. Bunker, who seemed not unwilling that his friend should find some entertaining distraction in St Egbert's, would look at the owners of these faces with a prospector's eye and his own unrivalled assurance.

They had walked up and down three or four times, when a desire for a different species of diversion began to overtake the Baron. It was the one kind of desire that the Baron never even tried to wrestle with.

"My vriend Bonker," said he, "is it not somevere about time for loncheon, eh?"

"I should say it was precisely the hour."

"Ha, ha! Zen, let us gom and eat. Himmel, zis sea is ze fellow to make von hungry!"

The Baron had taken a private suite of rooms on the first floor of the best hotel in St Egbert's, and after a very substantial lunch Mr. Bunker stretched himself on the luxurious sitting-room sofa and announced his intention of having a nap.

"I shall go out," said the Baron. "You vill not gom?"

"I shall leave you to make a single-handed conquest," replied Mr. Bunker. "Besides, I have a little matter I want to look into."

So the Baron arranged his hat airily, at what he had perceived to be the most fashionable and effective English angle, and strutted off to the esplanade.

It was about two hours later that he burst excitedly into the room, crying, "Aha, mine Bonker! I haf disgovered zomzing!" and then he stopped in some surprise. "Ello, vat make you, my vriend?"

His friend, in fact, seemed to be somewhat singularly employed. Through a dense cloud of tobacco-smoke you could just pick him out of the depths of an armchair, his feet resting on the mantelpiece, while his lap and all the floor round about were covered with immense books. The Baron's curiosity was still further excited by observing that they consisted principally of a London and a St Egbert's directory, several volumes of a Dictionary of National Biography, and one or two peerages and county family compilations.

He looked up with a smile. "You may well wonder, my dear Baron. The fact is, I am looking for a name."

"A name! Vat name?"

"Alas! If I knew what it was I should stop looking, and I confess I'm rather sick of the job."

"Vich vay do you look, zen?"

"Simply by wading my way through all the lists of names I could steal or borrow. It's devilish dry work."

"Ze name of a vriend, is it?"

"Yes; but I'm afraid I must wait till it comes. And what is this discovery, Baron? A petticoat, I presume. After all, they are the only things worth finding," and he shut the books one after another.

"A petticoat with ze fairest girl inside it!" exclaimed the Baron, rapturously.

"Your eyes seem to have been singularly penetrating, Baron. Was she dark or fair, tall or short, fat or slender, widow, wife, or maid?"

"Fair, viz blue eyes, short pairhaps but not too short, slender as a-a-drom-stick, and I vould say a maid; at least I see vun stout old lady mit her, mozzer and daughter I soppose."

"And did this piece of perfection seem to appreciate you?"

"Vy should I know? Zey are ze real ladies and pair tend not to see me, bot I zink zey notice me all ze same. Not 'lady vriends,' Bonker, ha, ha, ha!"

Mr. Bunker laughed with reminiscent amusement, and inquired, "And how did the romance end—in a cab, Baron?"

"Ha, ha, ha!" laughed the Baron; " better zan zat, Bonker—moch better!"

Mr. Bunker raised his eyebrows.

"It's hardly the time of year for a romance to end in a bathing-machine. You followed the divinity to her rented heaven, perhaps?"

The Baron bent forward and answered in a stage whisper, "Zey live in zis hotel, Bonker!"

"Then I can only wish you joy, Baron, and if my funds allow me, send her a wedding present."

"Ach, not quite so fast, my vriend! I am not caught so easy."

"My dear fellow, a week at close quarters is sufficient to net any man."

"Ven I marry," replied the Baron, "moch most be considered. A von Blitzenberg does not mate viz every vun."

"A good many families have made the same remark, but one does not always meet the fathers-in-law."

"Ha, ha! Ve shall see. Bot, Bonker, she is lofly!"

The Baron awaited dinner with even more than his usual ardour. He dressed with the greatest care, and at an absurdly early hour was already urging his friend to come down and take their places. Indeed after a time there was no withholding him, and they finally took their seats in the dining-room before anybody else.

At what seemed to the impatient Baron unconscionably long intervals a few people dropped in and began to study their menus and glance with an air of uncomfortable suspicion at their neighbours.

"I vonder vill she gom," he said three or four times at least.

"Console yourself, my dear Baron," his friend would reply; "they always come. That's seldom the difficulty."

And the Baron would dally with his victuals in the most unwonted fashion, and growl at the rapidity with which the courses followed one another.

"Do zey suppose ve vish to eat like—?" he began, and then laying his hand on his friend's sleeve, he whispered, "She goms!"

Mr. Bunker turned his head just in time to see in the doorway the Countess of Grillyer and the Lady Alicia à Fyre.

"Is she not fair?" asked the Baron, excitedly.

"I entirely approve of your taste, Baron. I have only once seen anyone quite like her before."

With a gratified smile the Baron filled his glass, while his friend seemed amused by some humorous reflection of his own.

The Lady Alicia and her mother had taken their seats at a table a little way off, and at first their eyes never happened to turn in the direction of the two friends. But at last, after looking at the ceiling, the carpet, the walls, the other people, everything else in the room it seemed, Lady Alicia's glance fell for an instant on the Baron. That nobleman looked as interesting as a mouthful of roast duck would permit him, but the glance passed serenely on to Mr. Bunker. For a moment it remained serene; suddenly it became startled and puzzled, and at that instant Mr. Bunker turned his own eyes full upon her, smiled slightly, and raised his glass to his lips.

The glance fell, and the Lady Alicia blushed down to the diamonds in her necklace.

The Baron insisted on lingering over his dinner till the charmer was finished, and so by a fortuitous coincidence they left the room immediately behind the Countess. The Baron passed them in the passage, and a few yards farther he looked round for his friend, and the Countess turned to look for her daughter.

They saw Lady Alicia following with an intensely unconscious expression, while Mr. Bunker was in the act of returning to the dining-room.

"I wanted to secure a table for breakfast," he explained.

CHAPTER II.

The Baron was in high hopes of seeing the fair unknown at breakfast, but it seemed she must be either breakfasting in her own room or lying long abed.

"I think I shall go out for a little constitutional," said Mr. Bunker, when he had finished. "I suppose the hotel has a stronger attraction for you."

"Ach, yes, I shall remain," his friend replied. "Pairhaps I may see zem."

"Take care then, Baron!"

"I shall not propose till you return, Bonker!"

"No," said Mr. Bunker to himself, "I don't think you will."

Just outside St Egbert's there is a high breezy sweep of downs, falling suddenly to a chalky seaward cliff. It overlooks the town and the undulating inland country and a great spread of shining sea; and even without a spy-glass you can see sail after sail and smoke-wreath after smoke-wreath go by all day long.

But Mr. Bunker had apparently walked there for other reasons than to see the view. He did stop once or twice, but it was only to scan the downs ahead, and at the sight of a fluttering skirt he showed no interest in anything else, but made a straight line for its owner. For her part, the lady seemed to await his coming. She gathered her countenance into an expression of as perfect unconcern as a little heightening of her colour would allow her, and returned his salute with rather a distant bow. But Mr. Bunker was not to be damped by this hint of barbed wire. He held out his hand and exclaimed cordially, "My dear Lady Alicia! This is charming of you!"

"Of course you understand, Mr. Beveridge, it's only—"

"Perfectly," he interrupted, gaily; "I understand everything I should and nothing I shouldn't. In fact, I have altered little, except in the trifling matter of a beard, a moustache or two, and, by the way, a name."

"A name?"

"I am now Francis Bunker, but as much at your service as ever."

"But why—I mean, have you really changed your name?"

"Circumstances have changed it, just as circumstances shaved me."

Lady Alicia made a great endeavour to look haughty. "I do not quite understand, Mr.—"

"Bunker—a temporary title, but suggestive, and simple for the tradesmen."

"I do not understand your conduct. Why have you changed your name?"

"Why not?"

This retort was so evidently unanswerable that Lady Alicia changed her inquiry.

"Where have you been?"

"Till yesterday, in London."

"Then you didn't go to your own parish?" she demanded, reproachfully.

"There were difficulties," he replied; "in fact, a certified lunatic is not in great demand as a parish priest. They seem to prefer them uncertified."

"But didn't you try?"

"Hard, but it was no use. The bishop was out of town, and I had to wait till his return; besides, my position was somewhat insecure. I have had at least two remarkable escapes since I saw you last."

"Are you safe here?" she asked, hurriedly.

"With your consent, yes."

She looked a little troubled. "I don't know that I am doing right, Mr. Bev—Bunker, but—"

"Thank you, my friend," he interrupted, tenderly.

"Don't," she began, hastily. "You mustn't talk like—"

"Francis Beveridge?" he interrupted. "The trouble is, this rascal Bunker bears an unconscionably awkward resemblance to our old friend."

"You must see that it is quite—ridiculous."

"Absurd," he agreed—"perfectly preposterous. I laugh whenever I think of it!"

Poor Lady Alicia felt like a man at a telephone who has been connected with the wrong person. Again she made a desperate shift to fall back on a becoming pride.

"What do you mean?" she demanded.

"If I mean anything at all, which is always rather doubtful," he replied, candidly, "I mean that Beveridge and his humbug were creatures of an occasion, just as Bunker and his are of another. The one occasion is passed, and with it the first entertaining gentleman has vanished into space. The second gentleman will doubtless follow when his time is up. In fact, I may be said to be a series of dissolving views."

"Then isn't what you said true?"

"I'm afraid you must be more specific; you see I've talked so much."

"What you said about yourself—and your work."

He shook his head humorously. "I have no means of checking my statements."

She looked at him in a troubled way, and then her eyes fell.

"At least," she said, "you won't—you mustn't treat me as—as you did."

"As Beveridge did? Certainly not; Bunker is the soul of circumspection. Besides, he doesn't require to get out of an asylum."

"Then it was only to get away?" she cried, turning scarlet.

"Let us call it so," he replied, looking pensively out to sea.

It seemed wiser to Lady Alicia to change the subject.

"Who is the friend you are staying with?" she asked, suddenly.

"My old friend the Baron Rudolph von Blitzenberg, and your own most recent admirer," he replied. "I am at present living with, in fact I may say upon, him."

"Does he know?"

"If you meet him, you had perhaps better not inquire into my past history."

"I meant, does he know about—about your knowing me?"

"Bless them!" thought Mr. Bunker; "one forgets they're not *always* thinking about us!"

"My noble friend has no idea that I have been so fortunate," he replied.

Lady Alicia looked relieved. "Who is he?" she asked.

"A German nobleman of great wealth, long descent, and the most accommodating disposition. He is at present exploring England under my guidance, and I flatter myself that he has already seen and done a number of things that are not on most programmes."

Lady Alicia was silent for a minute. Then she said with a little hesitation, "Didn't you get a letter from me?"

"A letter? No," he replied, in some surprise.

"I wrote twice—because you asked me to, and I thought—I wondered if you were safe."

"To what address did you write?"

"The address you gave me."

"And what was that?" he asked, still evidently puzzled.

"You said care of the Archbishop of York would find you."

Mr. Bunker abruptly looked the other way.

"By Jove!" he said, as if lost in speculation, "I must find out what the matter was. I can't imagine why they haven't been forwarded."

Lady Alicia appeared a little dissatisfied.

"Was that a *real* address?" she asked, suddenly.

"Perfectly," he replied; "as real as Pentonville Jail or the House of Commons." ("And as likely to find me," he added to himself.)

Lady Alicia seemed to hesitate whether to pursue the subject further, but in the middle of her debate Mr. Bunker asked, "By the way, has Lady Grillyer any recollection of having seen me before?"

"No, she doesn't remember you at all."

"Then we shall meet as strangers?"

"Yes, I think it would be better; don't you?"

"It will save our imaginations certainly."

Lady Alicia looked at him as though she expected something more; but as nothing came, she said, "I think it's time I went back."

"For the present then *au revoir,* my dear Alicia. I beg your pardon, Lady Alicia; it was that rascal Beveridge who made the slip. It now remains to make your formal acquaintance."

"You—you mustn't try!"

"The deuce is in these people beginning with B!" he laughed. "They seem to do things without trying."

He pressed her hand, raised his hat, and started back to the town. She, on her part, lingered to let him get a clear start of her, and her blue eyes looked as though a breeze had blown across and ruffled them.

Mr. Bunker had reached the esplanade, and was sauntering easily back towards the hotel, looking at the people and smiling now and then to himself, when he observed with considerable astonishment two familiar figures strolling towards him. They were none other than the Baron and the Countess, engaged in animated conversation, and apparently on the very best terms with each other. At the sight of him the Baron beamed joyfully.

"Aha, Bonker, so you haf returned!" he cried. "In ze meanvile I haf had vun great good fortune. Let me present my friend Mr. Bonker, ze Lady Grillyer."

The Countess bowed most graciously, and raising a pair of tortoise-shell-rimmed eye-glasses mounted on a stem of the same material, looked at Mr. Bunker through these with a by-no-means-disapproving glance.

At first sight it was evident that Lady Alicia must "take after" her noble father. The Countess was aquiline of nose, large of person, and emphatic in her voice and manner.

"You are the 'showman,' Mr. Bunker, are you not?" she said, with a smile for which many of her acquaintances would have given a tolerable percentage of their incomes.

"It seems," replied Mr. Bunker, smiling back agreeably, "that the Baron is now the showman, and I must congratulate him on his first venture."

For an instant the Countess seemed a trifle taken aback. It was a considerable number of years since she had been addressed in precisely this strain, and in fact at no time had her admirers ventured quite so dashingly to the attack. But there was something entirely irresistible in Mr. Bunker's manner, partly perhaps because he never made the mistake of heeding a first rebuff. The Countess coughed, then smiled a little again, and said to the Baron, "You didn't tell me that your showman supplied the little speeches as well."

"I could not know it; zere has not before been ze reason for a pretty speech," responded the Baron, gallantly.

If Lady Grillyer had been anybody else, one would have said that she actually giggled. Certainly a little wave of scandalised satisfaction rippled all over her.

"Oh, really!" she cried, "I don't know which of you is the worst offender."

All this time, as may be imagined, Mr. Bunker had been in a state of high mystification at his friend's unusual adroitness.

"How the deuce did he get hold of her?" he said to himself.

In the next pause the Baron solved the riddle.

"You vil vunder, Bonker," he said, "how I did gom to know ze Lady Grillyer."

"I envied, certainly," replied his friend, with a side glance at the now purring Countess.

"She vas of my introdogtions, bot till after you vent out zis morning I did not lairn her name. Zen I said to myself, 'Ze sun shines,

Himmel is kind! Here now is ze fair Lady Grillyer—my introdogtion!' And zo zat is how, you see."

"To think of the Baron being here and our only finding each other out by chance!" said the Countess.

"By a fortunate providence for me!" exclaimed the Baron, fervently.

"Baron," said the Countess, trying hard to look severe, "you must really keep some of these nice speeches for my daughter. Which reminds me, I wonder where she can be?"

"Ach, here she goms!" cried the Baron.

"Why, how did you know her?" asked the Countess.

"I—I did see her last night at dinnair," explained the Baron, turning red.

"Ah, of course, I remember," replied the Countess, in a matter-of-fact tone; but her motherly eye was sharp, and already it began to look on the highly eligible Rudolph with more approval than ever.

"My daughter Alicia, the Baron Rudolph von Blitzenberg, Mr. Bunker," she said the next moment.

The Baron went nearly double as he bowed, and the flourish of his hat stirred the dust on the esplanade. Mr. Bunker's salutation was less profound, but his face expressed an almost equal degree of interested respect. Her mother thought that when one of the gentlemen was a nobleman with an indefinite number of thousands a-year and the other a person of so much discrimination, Lady Alicia's own bow might have been a trifle less reserved. But then even the most astute mother cannot know the reasons for everything.

CHAPTER III.

"Alicia," said the Countess, "it was really a most fortunate coincidence our meeting the Baron at St Egbert's."

She paused for a reply and looked expectantly at her daughter. It was not the first time in the course of the morning that Lady Alicia had listened to similar observations, and perhaps that was why she answered somewhat listlessly, "Yes, wasn't it?"

The Countess frowned, and continued with emphasis, "I consider him one of the most agreeable and best informed young men I have ever met."

"Is he?" said Lady Alicia, absently.

"I wonder, Alicia, you hadn't noticed it," her mother observed, severely; "you talked with him most of the afternoon. I should have thought that no observant, well-bred girl would have failed to have been struck with his air and conversation."

"I—I thought him very pleasant, mamma."

"I am glad you had so much sense. He is extremely pleasant."

As Lady Alicia made no reply, the Countess felt obliged to continue his list of virtues herself.

"He is of most excellent family, Alicia, one of the oldest in Bavaria. I don't remember what I heard his income was in pfennigs, or whatever they measure money by in Germany, but I know that it is more than £20,000 a-year in English money. A very large sum nowadays," she added, as if £20,000 had grown since she was a girl.

"Yes, mamma."

"He is considered, besides, an unusually promising and intelligent young nobleman, and in Germany, where noblemen are still constantly used, that says a great deal for him."

"Does it, mamma?"

"Certainly it does. Education there is so severe that young Englishmen are beginning to know less than they ever did, and in most cases that isn't saying much. Compare the Baron with the young men you meet here!"

She looked at her daughter triumphantly, and Alicia could only reply, "Yes, mamma?"

"Compare them and see the difference. Look at the Baron's friend, Mr. Bunker, who is a very agreeable and amusing man, I admit, but look at the difference!"

"What is it?" Alicia could not help asking.

"*What* is it, Alicia! It is—ah—it's—er—it is, in short, the effect of a carefully cultivated mind and good blood."

"But don't you think Mr. Bunker cultivated, mamma—and—and—well-bred?"

"He has an amusing way of saying things—but then you must remember that the Baron is doubtless equally entertaining in his native language—and possibly a superficial knowledge of a few of the leading questions of the day; but the Baron talked to me for half an hour on the relations of something or other in Germany to—er—something else—a very important point, I assure you."

"I always thought him very clever," said Lady Alicia with a touch of warmth, and then instantly changed colour at the horrible slip.

"You always," said the Countess in alarmed astonishment; "you hardly spoke to him yesterday, and—had you met him before?"

"I—I meant the Baron, mamma."

"But I have just been saying that he was *unusually* clever."

"But I thought, I mean it seemed as though you considered him only well informed."

Lady Alicia's blushes and confusion deepened. Her mother looked at her with a softening eye. Suddenly she rose, kissed her affectionately, and said with the tenderness of triumph, "My *dear* girl! Of course he is; clever, well informed, and a most *desirable* young man. My Alicia could not do—"

She stopped, as if she thought this was perhaps a little premature (though the Countess's methods inclined to the summary and decisive), and again kissing her daughter affectionately, remarked gaily, "Let me see, why, it's almost time we went for our little walk! We mustn't really disappoint those young men. I am in the middle of such an amusing discussion with Mr. Bunker, who is really a very sensible man and quite worthy of the Baron's judgment."

Poor Lady Alicia hardly knew whether to feel more relieved at her escape or dismayed at the construction put upon her explanation. She went out to meet the Baron, determined to give no further colour to her mother's unlucky misconception. The Countess was far too experienced and determined a general to leave it at all doubtful who should walk by whose side, and who should have the opportunity of appreciating whose merits, but Lady Alicia was quite resolved that the Baron's blandishments should fall on stony ground.

But a soft heart and an undecided mouth are treacherous companions. The Baron was so amiable and so gallant, that at the end of half an hour she was obliged to abate the strictness of her resolution. She should treat him with the friendliness of a brother. She learned that he had no sisters: her decision was confirmed.

The enamoured and delighted Baron was in the seventh heaven of happy loquacity. He poured out particulars of his travels, his more recordable adventures, his opinions on various social and political matters, and at last even of the family ghost, the hereditary carpet-beatership, and the glories of Bavaria. And Lady Alicia listened with what he could not doubt was an interest touched with tenderness.

"I wonder," she said, artlessly, "that you find anything to admire in England—compared with Bavaria, I mean."

"Two zings I haf not zere," replied the Baron, waving his hand round towards the horizon. "Vun is ze vet sheet of flowing sea—says not your poet so? Ze ozzer" (laying his hand on his heart) "is ze Lady Alicia à Fyre."

There are some people who catch sentiment whenever it happens to be in the air, just as others almost equally unfortunate regularly take hay-fever.

Lady Alicia's reply was much softer than she intended, especially as she could have told anybody that the Baron's compliment was the merest figure of speech.

"You needn't have included me: I'm sure I'm not a great attraction."

"Ze sea is less, so zat leaves none," the Baron smiled.

"Didn't you see anybody—I mean, anything in London that attracted you—that you liked?"

"Zat I liked, yes, zat pairhaps for the moment attracted me; but not zat shall still attract me ven I am gone avay."

The Baron sighed this time, and she felt impelled to reply, with the most sisterly kindness, "I—we should, of course, like to think that you didn't forget us *altogether.*"

"You need not fear."

Then Lady Alicia began to realise that this was more like a second cousin than a brother, and with sudden sprightliness she cried, "I wonder where that steamer's going!"

The Baron turned his eyes towards his first-named attraction, but for a professed lover of the ocean his interest appeared slight. He only replied absently, "Ach, zo?"

A little way behind them walked Mr. Bunker and the Countess. The attention of Lady Grillyer was divided between the agreeable conversation of her companion and the pleasant spectacle of a fabulous number of pfennigs a-year bending its titled head over her daughter. In the middle of one of Mr. Bunker's most amusing stories she could not forbear interrupting with a complacent "They *do* make a very handsome couple!"

Mr. Bunker politely stopped his narrative, and looked critically from his friend's gaily checked back to Lady Alicia's trim figure.

"Pray go on with your story, Mr. Bunker," said the Countess, hastily, realising that she had thought a little too loudly.

"They are like," responded Mr. Bunker, replying to her first remark—"they are like a pair of gloves."

The Countess raised her brows and looked at him sharply.

"I mean, of course, the best quality."

"I think," said the Countess, suspiciously, "that you spoke a little carelessly."

"My simile was a little premature?"

"I think so," said the Countess, decisively.

"Let us call them then an odd pair," smiled Mr. Bunker, unruffled; "and only hope that they'll turn out to be the same size and different hands."

The Countess actually condescended to smile back.

"She is a *dear* child," she murmured.

"His income, I think, is sufficient," he answered.

Humour was not conspicuous in the Grillyer family. The Countess replied seriously, "I am one of those out-of-date people, Mr. Bunker, who consider some things come before money, but the Baron's birth and position are fortunately unimpeachable."

"While his mental qualities," said Mr. Bunker, "are, in my experience, almost unique."

The Countess was confirmed in her opinion of Mr. Bunker's discrimination.

Late that night, after they had parted with their friends, the Baron smoked in the most unwonted silence while Mr. Bunker dozed on the sofa. Several times Rudolph threw restive glances at his friend, as if he had something on his mind that he needed a helping hand to unburden himself of. At last the silence grew so intolerable that he screwed up his courage and with desperate resolution exclaimed, "Bonker!"

Mr. Bunker opened his eyes and sat up.

"Bonker, I am in loff!"

Mr. Bunker smiled and stretched himself out again.

"I have also been in love," he replied.

"You are not now?"

"Alas! no."

"Vy alas?"

"Because follies *without* illusions get so infernally dull, Baron."

The Baron smiled a little foolishly.

"I haf ze illusions, I fear." Then he broke out enthusiastically, "Ach, bot is she not lofly, Bonker? If she will bot lof me back I shall be ze happiest man out of heaven!"

"You have wasted no time, Baron."

The Baron shook his head in melancholy pleasure.

"You are quite sure it is really love this time?" his friend pursued.

"Qvite!" said the Baron, with the firmness of a martyr.

"There are so many imitations."

"Not so close zat zey can deceive!"

"Ha, ha, ha!" laughed Mr. Bunker. "These first symptoms are common to them all, and yet the varieties of the disease are almost beyond counting. I myself have suffered from it in eight different forms. There was the virulent, spotted-all-over variety, known as calf-love; there was the kind that accompanied itself by a course of the Restoration dramatists; another form I may call the strayed-Platonic, and that may be subdivided into at least two; then there was—"

"Schtop! schtop!" cried the Baron. "Ha, ha, ha! Zat will do! Teufel! I most examine my heart strictly. And yet, Bonker, I zink my loff is anozzer kind—ze *real!*"

"They are all that, Baron; but have it your own way. Anything I can do to make you worse shall be done."

"Zanks, my best of friends," said the Baron, warmly, seizing his hand; "I knew you would stand by me!"

Mr. Bunker gave a little laugh, and returning the pressure, replied, "My dear fellow, I'd do anything to oblige a friend in such an interesting condition."

CHAPTER IV.

The Baron was a few minutes late in joining the party at lunch, and when he appeared he held an open letter in his hand. It was only the middle of the next day, and yet he could have sworn that last night he was comparatively whole-hearted, he felt so very much more in love already.

"Yet anozzer introdogtion has found me out," he said as he took his seat. "I have here a letter of invitation vich I do not zink I shall accept."

He threw an amorous glance at Lady Alicia, which her watchful mother rightly interpreted as indicating the cause of his intended refusal.

"Who is it this time?" asked Mr. Bunker.

"Sir Richard Brierley of Brierley Park, Dampshire. Is zat how you pronounce it?"

"Sir Richard Brierley!" exclaimed the Countess; "why, Alicia and I are going to visit some relatives of ours who live only six miles from Brierley Park! When has he asked you, Baron?"

"Ze end of next week."

"How odd! We are going down to Dampshire at the end of next week too. You must accept, Baron!"

"I shall!" exclaimed the overjoyed Baron. "Shall ve go, Bonker?"

"I'm not asked, I'm afraid."

"Ach, bot zat is nozzing. I shall tell him."

"As you please, Baron," replied Mr. Bunker, with a half glance at Lady Alicia.

The infatuated Baron had already begun to dread the inevitable hour of separation, and this piece of good fortune put him into the highest spirits. He felt so amiable towards the whole world that when the four went out for a stroll in the afternoon he lingered for a minute by Lady Grillyer's side, and in that minute Mr. Bunker and Lady Alicia were out of hail ahead. The Baron's face fell.

"Shall I come down to this place?" said Mr. Bunker.

"Would you like to?"

"I should be sorry," he replied, "to part with—the Baron."

Lady Alicia had expected a slightly different ending to this sentence, and so, to tell the truth, Mr. Bunker had intended.

"Oh, if you can't stay away from the Baron, you had better go."

"It is certainly very hard to tear myself away from so charming a person as the Baron; perhaps you can feel for me?"

"I think he is very—nice."

"He thinks you very nice."

"Does he?" said Lady Alicia, with great indifference, and a moment later changed the subject.

Meanwhile the Baron was growing very uneasy. Of course it was quite natural that Mr. Bunker should find it pleasant to walk for a few minutes by the side of the fairest creature on earth, and very possibly he was artfully pleading his friend's cause. Yet the Baron felt uneasy. He remembered Mr. Bunker's invariable success with the gentler sex, his wit, his happy smile, and his good looks; and he began to wish most sincerely that these fascinations were being exercised on the now somewhat breathless Countess, for his efforts to overtake the pair in front had both annoyed and exhausted Lady Grillyer.

"Need we walk quite so fast, Baron?" she suggested; and Lady Grillyer's suggestions were of the kind that are evidently meant to be acted upon.

"Ach, I did forged," said the Baron, absently, and without further remark he slackened his pace for a few yards and then was off again.

"You were telling me," gasped the Countess, "of something you thought of—doing when—you went—home."

"Zo? Oh yes, it vas—Teufel! I do not remember."

"Really, Baron," said the Countess, decidedly, "I cannot go any farther at this rate. Let us turn. The others will be turning too, in a minute."

In fact the unlucky Baron had clean run Lady Grillyer's maternal instincts off their feet, and he suffered for it by seeing nothing of either his friend or his charmer for an hour and a half.

That night he accepted Sir Richard's invitation, but said nothing whatever about bringing a friend.

For the next week Rudolph was in as many states of mind as there were hours in each day. He walked and rode and drove with Lady Alicia through the most romantic spots he could find. He purchased a large assortment of golf-clubs, and under her tuition essayed to play that most dangerous of games for mixed couples. In turn he broke every club in his set; the cavities he hewed in the links are still pointed out to the curious; but the heart of the Lady Alicia alone he seemed unable to damage. There was always a moment at which his courage failed him, and in that fatal pause she invariably changed the subject with the most innocent air in the world.

Every now and then the greenest spasms of jealousy would seize him. Why did she elect to disappear with Mr. Bunker on the very morning that he had resolved should settle his fate? It is true he had made the same resolution every morning, but on this particular one he had no doubt he would have put his fate to the touch. And why on a certain moonlight evening was he left to the unsentimental company of the Countess?

He made no further reference to the visit to Brierley Park; in fact he shunned discussion of any kind with his quondam bosom friend.

The time slipped past, till the visit to St Egbert's was almost at an end. On the day after tomorrow all four were going to leave (where Mr. Bunker was going, his friend never troubled to inquire).

They sat together lateish in the evening in the Baron's room. That very afternoon Lady Alicia had spent more time in Mr. Bunker's society than in his, and the Baron felt that the hour had come for an explanation.

"Bonker, I haf a suspection!" he exclaimed, suddenly. "It is not I, bot you, who are ze friend to ze beautiful Lady Alicia. You are not doing me fair!"

"My dear Baron!"

"It is so: you are not doing me fair," the Baron reiterated.

"My dear fellow," replied Mr. Bunker, "it is you are so much in love that you have lost your wonted courage. You don't use your chances."

"I do not get zem."

"Nonsense, Baron! I haven't spent one hour in Lady Alicia's company to your twenty-four, and yet if I'd been matrimonially inclined I could have proposed twice over. You've had the chance of being accepted fifty times."

"I haf not been accepted vunce," said the Baron, moodily.

"Have you put the question?"

"I haf not dared."

"Well, my dear Baron, whose fault is that?"

The Baron was silent.

"Ask her tomorrow."

"No, Bonker," said the Baron, sadly; "she treats me not like a lover. She talks of friendship. I do not vish a frient!"

Mr. Bunker looked thoughtfully up at the ceiling. "You don't think you have touched her heart?" he asked at length.

"I fear not."

"You must try an infallible recipe for winning a woman's heart. You must be in trouble."

"In trouble!"

"I have tried it once myself, with great success."

"Bot how?"

"You must fall ill."

"Bot I cannot; I am too healthful, alas!"

Mr. Bunker smiled artfully. "They come to tea in our rooms tomorrow, you know. By then, Baron, you must be laid up, ill or not, just as you please. A grain of Lady Alicia's sympathy is worth more than a ton of even your wit."

The standard chosen for the measurement of his wit escaping the Baron, the scheme delighted him.

"Ha, Bonker! schön! I tvig! Goot!" he cried. "How shall ve do?"

"Leave it to me."

The Baron reflected, and his smile died away.

"Sopposing," he said, slowly, "zey find out? Is it vise? Is it straight?"

"They can't find out. They go the next morning, and what's to prevent your making a quick recovery and pluckily going down to Brierley Park as the interesting convalescent? She will know that you've made a dangerous journey on her account."

The Baron's face cleared again.

"Let us try!" he said; "anyzing is better zan my present state. Bot, be careful, Bonker!"

"I shall take the most minute precautions," replied Mr. Bunker.

CHAPTER V.

The next morning the two conspirators breakfasted early. The Baron seemed a little nervous now that it came so near the venture, but his friend was as cheerful as a schoolboy, and his confident air soon put fresh courage into Rudolph.

Mr. Bunker's bedroom opened out of their common sitting-room, and so he declared that in the afternoon the Baron must be laid up there.

"Keep your room all morning," he said, "and look as pale as you can. I shall make my room ready for you."

When the Baron had retired, he threw himself into a chair and gazed for a few minutes round his bedroom. Then he rang his bell, ordered the servant to make the bed immediately, and presently went out to do some shopping. On the way he sent word to the Countess, telling her only that the Baron was indisposed, but that in spite of this misfortune he hoped he should have the pleasure of their company at tea. The rest of the morning he spent in his bedroom, prudently keeping out of the ladies' way.

When, after a substantial lunch which he insisted upon getting up to eat, the Baron was allowed to enter the sick-room, he uttered an exclamation of astonishment—and indeed his surprise was natural. The room was as full of flowers as a conservatory; chairs, wardrobe, and fireplace were most artistically draped with art hangings; a plate filled with grapes, a large bottle labelled "Two table-spoonfuls every half hour," and a medicine-glass were placed conspicuously on a small table; and, most remarkable feature of all, Mr. Bunker's bath filled with water and alive with goldfish stood by the side of the bed. A couple of canaries sang in a cage by the window, the half-drawn curtains only permitted the most delicate light to steal into the room, and in short the whole arrangement reflected the utmost credit on his ingenious friend.

The Baron was delighted, but a little puzzled.

"Vat for are zese fishes and ze canaries?" he asked.

"To show your love of nature."

"Vy so?"

"There is nothing that pleases a woman more."

"My friend, you zink of everyzing!" exclaimed the Baron, admiringly.

When four o'clock approached he drew a night-shirt over his other garments and got into bed. Mr. Bunker at first was in favour of a complete change of attire, but on his friend's expostulating against such a thorough precaution, he admitted that it would be perhaps rather like the historic blacking of Othello.

"Leave it all to me, my dear Baron," he said, reassuringly, as he tucked him in; and with that he went into the other room and awaited the arrival of their guests.

They came punctually. The Countess was full of concern for the "dear Baron," while Lady Alicia, he could not help thinking, appeared unusually reserved. In fact, his quick eye soon divined that something was the matter.

"She has either been getting a lecture from the dowager or has found something out," he said to himself.

However, it seemed that if she had found anything out it could have nothing to do with the Baron's indisposition, for she displayed the most ingenuous sympathy, and, he thought, she even appeared to aim it pointedly at himself.

"So sudden!" exclaimed the Countess.

"It is rather sudden, but we'll hope it may pass as quickly as it came," said Mr. Bunker, conveying a skilful impression of deep concern veiled by a cheerful manner.

"Tell me honestly, Mr. Bunker, is it dangerous?" demanded the Countess.

Mr. Bunker hesitated, gave a half-hearted laugh, and replied, "Oh, dear, no! That is—at present, Lady Grillyer, we have really no reason to be alarmed."

"I am *so* sorry," murmured Lady Alicia.

Her mother looked at her approvingly.

"Poor Baron!" she said, in a tone of the greatest commiseration.

"So far from home!" sighed Mr. Bunker. "And yet so cheerful through it all," he added.

"What did you say was the matter?" asked the Countess.

Mr. Bunker had thought it both wiser and more effective to maintain a little mystery round his friend's malady.

"The doctor hasn't yet given a decided opinion," he replied.

"Can't we do anything?" said Lady Alicia, softly.

Mr. Bunker thought the guests were nearly worked up to the proper pitch of sympathy.

"Poor Rudolph!" he exclaimed. "It would cheer him immensely, I know, and ease my own anxiety as well, if you would venture in to see him for a few minutes. In such a case there is no sympathy so welcome as a woman's."

The Countess glanced at her daughter, and wavered for an instant between those proprieties for which she was a famous stickler and this admirable chance of completing the Baron's conquest.

"His relations are far away," said Mr. Bunker, looking pensively out of the window.

"We might come in for a few minutes, Alicia?" suggested Lady Grillyer.

"Yes, mamma," replied Lady Alicia, with an alacrity that rather surprised their host.

With a pleasantly dejected air he ushered the ladies into the darkened sick-room. The Baron, striving to conceal his exultation under a rueful semblance, greeted them with a languid yet happy smile.

"Ah, Lady Grillyer, zis is kind indeed! And you, Lady Alicia, how can I zank you?"

"My daughter and I are much distressed, Baron, to find our host *hors de combat,*" said the Countess, graciously.

"Just when you wanted to go away too!" added Lady Alicia, sympathetically.

The Baron emitted a happy blend of sigh and groan.

"Alas!" he replied, "it is hard indeed."

"You must hurry up and get better," said the Countess, in her most cheering sick-room manner. "It won't do to disappoint the Brierleys, you know."

"You must come down for *part* of the time," smiled her daughter.

These expressions of sympathy so affected the Baron that he placed his hand on his brow and turned slightly away to conceal his emotion. At the same time Mr. Bunker, with well-timed dramatic effect, sank wearily into a chair, and, laying his elbow on the back, hid his own face in his hand.

Their guests jumped to the most alarming conclusions, and looked from one to the other with great concern.

"Dear me!" said the Countess, "surely it isn't so very serious, Mr. Bunker; it isn't *infectious,* is it?"

The unlucky Baron here made his first mistake: without waiting for his more diplomatic friend to reply, he answered hastily, "Ach, no, it is bot a cold."

Lady Grillyer's expression changed.

"A cold!" she said. "Dear me, that can't be so very serious, Baron."

"It is a bad cold," said the Baron.

By this time the ladies' eyes were growing more used to the dim light, and Mr. Bunker could see that they were taking rapid stock of the garnishings.

"This, I suppose, is your cough-mixture," said the Countess, examining the bottle.

The Baron incautiously admitted it was.

"Two table-spoonfuls every half hour!" she exclaimed; "why, I never heard of taking a cough-mixture in such doses. Besides, your cough doesn't seem so very bad, Baron."

"Ze doctor told me to take it so," replied the Baron.

The Countess turned towards Mr. Bunker and said, with a touch of suspicion in her voice, "I thought, Mr. Bunker, the doctor had given no opinion."

The Baron threw a glance of intense ferocity at his friend.

"In the Baron's desire to spare your feelings," replied Mr. Bunker, gravely, "he has been a little inaccurate; that is not precisely an ordinary cough-mixture."

"Oh," said the Countess.

Lady Alicia's attention had been strongly attracted by the bath, and suddenly she exclaimed, "Why, there are goldfish in it!"

The Baron's nerve was fast deserting him.

"Ze doctor ordered zem," he began—"I mean, I am fond of fishes."

The Countess looked hard at the unhappy young man, and then turned severely to his friend.

"*What* is the matter with the Baron?" she demanded.

Mr. Bunker saw there was nothing for it but heroic measures.

"The dog was destroyed at once," he replied, with intense gravity. "It is therefore impossible to say exactly what is the matter."

"*The dog!*" cried the two ladies together.

"By this evening," he continued, "we shall know the worst—or the best."

"What do you mean?" exclaimed the Countess, withdrawing a step from the bed.

"I mean," replied Mr. Bunker, with a happy inspiration, "that this bath is a delicate test. No victim of the dread disease of hydrophobia can bear to look—"

But the Countess gave him no time to finish. Even as he was

speaking the Baron's face had passed through a series of the most extraordinary expressions, which she not unnaturally put down to premonitory symptoms.

"It's beginning already!" she shrieked. "Alicia, my love, come quickly. How dare you expose us, sir?"

"Calm yourselves. I assure you—" pleaded Mr. Bunker, coming hastily after them, but they were at the door before him.

The hapless Baron could stand it no longer. Crying, "No, no, it is false!" he sprang out of bed, arrayed in a tweed suit only half concealed by his night-shirt, and, forgetting all about the bath, descended with a great splash among the startled goldfish.

The Countess paused in the half-opened door and looked at him with horror that rapidly passed into intense indignation.

"I am not ill!" he cried. "It vos zat rascal Bonker's plot. He made me! I haf not hydrophobia!"

Most unkindest cut of all, Lady Alicia went off into hysterical giggles. For a moment her mother glared at the two young men in silence, and then only remarking, "I have never been so insulted before," she went out, and her daughter followed her.

As the door closed Mr. Bunker went off into roar after roar of laughter, but the humorous side of the situation seemed to appeal very slightly to his injured friend.

"You rascal! You villain!" he shouted, "zis is ze end of our friendship, Bonker! Do you use ze pistols? Tell me, sare!"

"My dear Baron," gasped Mr. Bunker, "I could not put such an inartistic end to so fine a joke for the world."

"You vill not fight? Coward! Poltroon! I know not ze English name bad enoff for you!"

With difficulty Mr. Bunker composed himself and replied, still smiling: "After all, Baron, what harm has been done? I get all the blame, and the sympathy you wanted is sure to turn to you."

"False friend!" thundered the Baron.

"My dear Baron!" said Mr. Bunker, mildly, "whose fault was it that the plot miscarried? If you'd only left it all to me—"

"Left it to you! Yes, I left too moch to you! Traitor, it vas a trick to vin ze Lady Alicia for yourself! Speak to me nevermore!" And with that the infuriated nobleman rushed off to his own room.

As there was no further sign of him for the next half hour, Mr. Bunker, still smiling to himself at the recollection, went out to take the air; but just as he was about to descend the stairs he spied Lady Alicia lingering in a passage. He turned back and went up to her.

She began at once in a low, hurried voice that seemed to have a strain of anger running beneath it.

"I got the two letters I wrote you returned to me today through the dead-letter office. Nothing was known about you at the address you gave."

"I am not surprised," he replied.

"Then it was false?"

"As an address it was perfectly genuine, only it didn't happen to be mine."

"Were you *ever* in the Church?"

"Not to my personal knowledge."

"Yet you said you were?"

"I was in an asylum."

She looked up at him with fine contempt, while he smiled back at her with great amusement.

"You have deceived *me,*" she said, "and you have treated your other friend—who is far too good for you—disgracefully. Have you anything to say for yourself?"

"Not a word," he replied, cheerfully.

"You must never treat me again as—as I let you."

As a smile played for an instant about his face, she added quickly, "I don't *suppose* I shall ever see you again. In future we are not *likely* to meet."

"The lady and the lunatic?" said he. "Well, perhaps not. Good-bye, and better luck."

"Good-bye," she answered coldly, and added as they parted, "my mother, of course, is extremely angry with you."

"There," he said with a smile, "you see I still come in useful."

She hurried away, and Mr. Bunker walked slowly downstairs and out of the hotel.

"It seems to me," he reflected, "that I shall have to set out on my adventures again alone."

CHAPTER VI.

The Baron's natural good temper might have forgiven his friend, but all night he was a prey to something against which no temper is proof. The Baron was bitterly jealous. All through breakfast he never spoke a word, and when Mr. Bunker asked him what train he intended to take, he replied curtly, as he went to the door, "Ze 5.30."

"And where do you go now?"

"Vat is zat to you? I go for a valk. I vould be alone."

"Good-bye, then, Baron," said Mr. Bunker. "I think I shall go up to town."

"Go, zen," replied the Baron, opening the door; "I haf no furzer vish to see a treacherous *sponge* zat vill neizer be true nor fight, bot jost takes money."

He slammed the door and went out. If he had waited for a moment, he would have seen a look in Mr. Bunker's face that he had never seen before. He half started from his chair to follow, and then sat down again and thought with his lips very tight set.

All at once they broke into a smile that was grimmer than anything the Baron had known.

"I accept your challenge, Baron Rudolph von Blitzenberg," he said to himself; "but the weapons I shall choose myself."

He took a telegraph form, wrote and despatched a wire, and then with considerable haste proceeded to pack. Within an hour he had left the hotel.

When a servant, later in the day, was performing, under the Baron's directions, the same office for him, a series of discoveries that still further disturbed his peace of mind were jointly made. Not only the more sporting portions of his wardrobe but his gun and cartridges as well had vanished, and, search and storm as he liked, there was not a trace of them to be found.

"Ze rascal!" he muttered; "I did not zink he was zief as well."

It is hardly wonderful that he arrived at Brierley station in anything but an amiable frame of mind. There, to his great annoyance and surprise, he found no signs of Sir Richard's carriage; there were no stables near, and, after fuming for some time on the platform, he was forced to leave his luggage with the station-master and proceed on foot to Brierley Park.

He arrived shortly before seven o'clock, after a dark and muddy tramp, and, still swearing under his breath, pulled the bell with indignant energy.

"I am ze Baron von Blitzenberg, bot zere vas no carriage at ze station," he informed the butler in his haughtiest tones.

The man looked at him suspiciously.

"The Baron arrived this morning," he said.

"Ze Baron? Vat Baron? I am ze Baron!"

"I shall fetch Sir Richard," said the butler, turning away.

Presently a stout florid gentleman, accompanied by three friends, all evidently very curious and amused about something, came to the door, and, to the poor Baron's amazement and horror, he recognised in one of these none other than Mr. Bunker, arrayed with much splendour in his own ornate shooting suit.

"What do you want?" asked the florid gentleman, sternly.

"Have I ze pleasure of addressing Sir Richard Brierley?" inquired the Baron, raising his hat and bowing profoundly.

"You have."

"Zen I must tell you zat I am ze Baron Rudolph von Blitzenberg."

"Gom, gom, my man!" interposed Mr. Bunker. "I know you. Zis man, Sir Richard, has before annoyed me. He is vat you call impostor, cracked; he has vollowed me from Germany. Go avay, man!"

"You are impostor! You scoundrel, Bonker!" shouted the wrathful Baron. "He is no Baron, Sir Richard! Ha! Vould you again deceive me, Bonker?"

"You must lock him up, I fear," said Mr. Bunker. "Tomorrow, my man, you vill see ze police."

So completely did the Baron lose his head that he became almost inarticulate with rage: his protestations, however, were not of the slightest avail. That morning Sir Richard had received a wire informing him that the Baron was coming by an earlier train than he had originally intended, and, since his arrival, the spurious nobleman had so ingratiated himself with his host that Sir Richard was filled with nothing but sympathy for him in his persecution. After a desperate struggle the unfortunate Rudolph was overpowered and conveyed in the undignified fashion known as the frog's march to a room in a remote wing, there to pass the night under lock and key.

"The scoundrelly German impostor!" exclaimed a young man, a fellow visitor of the Baron Bunker's, to a tall, military-looking gentleman.

Colonel Savage seemed lost in thought.

"It is a curious thing, Trelawney," he replied, at length, "that the footman who attends the Baron should have told my man—who, of course, told me—that a number of his things are marked 'Francis Beveridge.' It is also rather strange that this impostor should have known so little of the Baron's movements as to arrive several hours after him, assuming he had hatched a plot to impersonate him."

"But the man's obviously mad."

"Must be," said the colonel.

The house party was assembled in the drawing-room waiting for dinner to be announced. The bogus Baron was engaged in an animated discussion with Colonel Savage on the subject of Bavarian shootings, and the colonel having omitted to inform him that he had some personal experience of these, Mr. Bunker was serving up such of his friend's anecdotes as he could remember with sauce more peculiarly his own.

"Five hondred vild boars," he was saying, "eight hondred brace of partridges, many bears, and rabbits so moch zat it took five veeks to bury zem. All zese ve did shoot before breakfast, colonel. Aftair breakfast again ve did go out—"

But at that moment his attention was sharply arrested by a question of Lady Brierley's.

"Has Dr. Escott arrived?" she asked.

The Baron Bunker paused, and in spite of his habitual coolness, the observant colonel noticed that he started ever so slightly.

"He came half an hour ago," replied Sir Richard. "Ah, here he is."

As he spoke, a well-remembered figure came into the room, and after a welcome from his hostess, the dinner procession started.

"Whoever is that tall fair man in front?" Dr. Escott asked his partner as they crossed the hall.

"Oh, that's the Baron von Blitzenberg: such an amusing man! We are all in love with him already."

All through dinner the spurious Baron saw that Dr. Escott's eyes turned continually and curiously on him; yet never for an instant did his spirits droop or his conversation flag. Witty and charming as ever, he discoursed in his comical foreign accent to the amusement of all within hearing, and by the time the gentlemen adjourned to the billiard-room, he had established the reputation of being the most delightful German ever seen. Yet Dr. Escott grew more suspicious and bewildered, and Mr. Bunker felt that he was being narrowly watched. The skill at billiards of a certain Francis Beveridge used to be the object of the doctor's unbounded admiration, and it was with the liveliest interest that he watched a game between Colonel Savage and the Baron.

That nobleman knew well the danger of displaying his old dexterity, and to the onlookers it soon became apparent that this branch of his education had been neglected. He not only missed the simplest shots, but seemed very ignorant of the rules of the English game, and in consequence he came in for a little good-natured chaff from Sir Richard and Trelawney. When the colonel's score stood at 90 and the Baron had scarcely reached 25 Trelawney cried, "I'll bet you ten to one you don't win, Baron!"

"What in?" asked the Baron, and the colonel noticed that for the first time he pronounced a *w* correctly.

"Sovereigns," said Trelawney, gaily.

The temptation was irresistible.

"Done!" said the Baron. With a professional disregard for conventions he bolted the white into the middle pocket, leaving his own ball nicely beside the red. Down in its turn went the red, and Mr. Bunker was on the spot. Three followed three in monotonous succession, Trelawney's face growing longer and Dr. Escott getting more and more excited, till with a smile Mr. Bunker laid down his cue, a sensational winner.

His victory was received in silence: Trelawney handed over two five-pound notes without a word, and the colonel returned to his whisky-and-soda. Dr. Escott could contain himself no longer, and whispering something to Sir Richard, the two left the room.

Imperturbable as ever, Mr. Bunker talked gaily for a few minutes to an unresponsive audience, and then, remarking that he would join the ladies, left the room.

A minute or two later Sir Richard, with an anxious face, returned with Dr. Escott.

"Where is the Baron?" he asked.

"Gone to join the ladies," replied Trelawney, adding under his breath, "d—n him!"

But the Baron was not with the ladies, nor, search the house as they might, was there a trace to be seen of that accomplished nobleman.

"He has gone!" said Sir Richard.

"What the deuce is the meaning of it?" exclaimed Trelawney.

Colonel Savage smiled grimly and suggested, "Perhaps he wants to give the impostor an innings."

"Dr. Escott, I think, can tell you," replied the baronet.

"Gentlemen," said the doctor, "the man whom you have met as the Baron von Blitzenberg is none other than a most cunning and determined lunatic. He escaped from the asylum where I am at present assistant doctor, after all but murdering me; he has been seen in London since, but how he came to impersonate the unfortunate gentleman whom you locked up this afternoon I cannot say."

Before they broke up for the night the genuine Baron, released from confinement and soothed by the humblest apologies and a heavy supper, recounted the main events in Mr. Beveridge *alias* Bunker's brief career in town. On his exploits in St Egbert's he felt some delicacy in touching, but at the end of what was after all only a fragmentary and one-sided narrative, even the defrauded Trelawney could not but admit that, whatever the departed gentleman's failings, his talents at least were worthy of a better cause.

CHAPTER VII.

The party at Brierley Park had gone at last to bed. The Baron was installed in his late usurper's room, and from the clock-tower the hour of three had just been tolled. Sympathy and Sir Richard's cellar had greatly mollified the Baron's wrath; he had almost begun to see the humorous side of his late experience; as a rival Mr. Bunker was extinct, and with an easy mind and a placid smile he had fallen asleep some two hours past.

The fire burned low, and for long nothing but the occasional sigh of the wind in the trees disturbed the silence. At length, had the Baron been awake, he might have heard the stealthiest of footsteps in the corridor outside. Then they stopped; his door was gently opened, and first a head and then a whole man slipped in.

Still the Baron slept, dreaming peacefully of his late companion. They were driving somewhere in a hansom, Mr. Bunker was telling one of his most amusing stories, when there came a shock, the hansom seemed to turn a somersault, and the Baron awoke. At first he thought he must be dreaming still; the electric light had been turned on and the room was bright as day, but, more bewildering yet, Mr. Bunker was seated on his bed, gazing at him with an expression of thoughtful amusement.

"Well, Baron," he said, "I trust you are comfortable in these excellent quarters."

The Baron, half awake and wholly astonished, was unable to collect his ideas in time to make any reply.

"But remember," continued Mr. Bunker, "you have a reputation to live up to. I have set the standard high for Bavarian barons."

The indignant Baron at last recovered his wits.

"If you do not go away *at vonce,*" he said, raising himself on his elbows, "I shall raise ze house upon you!"

"Have you forgotten that you are talking to a dangerous lunatic, who probably never stirs without his razor?"

The Baron looked at him and turned a little pale. He made no further movement, but answered stoutly enough, "Vat do you vant?"

"In the first place, I want my brush and comb, a few clothes, and my hand-bag. Events happened rather more quickly this evening than I had anticipated."

"Take zem."

"I should also like," continued Mr. Bunker, unmoved, "to have a little talk with you. I think I owe you some explanation—perhaps an apology or two—and I'm afraid it's my last chance."

"Zay it zen."

"Of course I understand that you make no hostile demonstration till I am finished? A hunted man must take precautions, you know."

"I vill let you go."

"Thanks, Baron."

Mr. Bunker folded his arms, leaned his back against the foot of the bed, and began in his half-bantering way, "I have amused you, Baron, now and then, you must admit?"

The Baron made no reply.

"That I place to my credit, and I think few debts are better worth repaying. On the other hand, I confess I have subsisted for some time entirely on your kindness. I'm afraid that alone counterbalances the debt, and when it comes to my being the means of your taking a bath in mixed company and spending an evening in a locked room, there's no doubt the balance is greatly on your side."

"I zink so," observed the Baron.

"So I'll tell you a true story, a favour with which I haven't indulged anyone for some considerable time."

The Baron coughed, but said nothing.

"My biography for all practical purposes," Mr. Bunker continued, "begins in that sequestered retreat, Clankwood Asylum. How and with whom I came there I haven't the very faintest recollection. I simply woke up from an extraordinary drowsiness to find myself recovering from a sharp attack of what I may most euphoniously call mental excitement. The original cause of it is very dim in my mind, and has, so far as I remember, nothing to do with the rest of the story. The attack was very short, I believe. I soon came to something more or less like myself; only, Baron, the singular thing is, that it was to all intents and purposes a new self—whether better or worse, my faulty memory does not permit me to say. I'd clean forgotten who I was and all about me. I found myself called Francis Beveridge, but that wasn't my old name, I know."

"Ha!" exclaimed the Baron, growing interested despite himself.

"And the most remarkable thing of all is that up till this day I haven't the very vaguest notion what my real name is."

"Zo?" said the Baron. "Bot vy should they change it?"

"There you've laid your finger on the mystery, Baron. Why? Heaven knows: I wish I did!"

The Baron looked at him with undisguised interest.

"Strange!" he said, thoughtfully.

"Damnably strange. I found myself compelled to live in an asylum and answer to a new name, and really, don't you know, under the circumstances I could give no very valid reason for getting out. I seemed to have blossomed there like one of the asylum plants. I couldn't possibly have been more identified with the place. Besides, I'm free to confess that for some time my reason, taking it all in all, wasn't particularly valid on any point. By George, I had a funny time! Ha, ha, ha!"

His mirth was so infectious that the Baron raised his voice in a hearty "Ha, ha!" and then stopped abruptly, and said cautiously, "Haf a care, Bonker, zey may hear!"

"However, Baron," Mr. Bunker continued, "out I was determined to get, and out I came in the manner of which perhaps my friend Escott has already informed you."

The Baron grinned and nodded.

"I came up to town, and on my very first evening I had the good fortune to meet the Baron Rudolph von Blitzenberg—as perhaps you may remember. In my own defence, Baron, I may fairly plead that since I could remember nothing about my past career, I was entitled to supply the details from my imagination. After all, I have no proof that some of my stories may not have been correct. I used this privilege freely in Clankwood, and, in a word, since I couldn't tell the truth if I wanted to, I quenched the desire."

"You hombog!" said the Baron, not without a note of admiration.

"I was, and I gloried in it. Baron, if you ever want to know how ample a thing life can be, become a certified lunatic! You are quite irresponsible for your debts, your crimes, and, not least, your words. It certainly enlarges one's horizon. All this time, I may say, I was racking my brains—which, by the way, have been steadily growing saner in other matters—for some recollections of my previous whereabouts, my career, if I had any, and, above all, of my name."

"Can you remember nozing?"

"I can remember a large country house which I think belonged to me, but in what part of the country it stands I haven't the slightest recollection. I can't remember any family, and as no one has inquired for me, I don't suppose I had any. Many incidents—sporting, festive, amusing, and discreditable—I remember distinctly, and many faces, but there's nothing to piece them together with. Can you recall one or two incidents in town, when people spoke to me or bowed to me?"

"Yes, vell; I vondered zen."

"I suppose they knew me. In a general sort of way I knew them. But when a man doesn't know his own name, and will probably be replaced in an asylum if he's identified, there isn't much encouragement for greeting old friends. And do you remember my search for a name in the hotel at St Egbert's?"

"Yah—zat is, yes."

"It was for my own I was looking."

"You found it not?"

"No. The worst of it is, I can't even remember what letter it began with. Sometimes I think it was M, or perhaps N, and sometimes I'm almost sure it was E. It will come to me someday, no doubt, Baron, but till it does I shall have to wander about a nameless man, looking for it. And after all, I am not without the consolations of a certain useful, workaday kind of philosophy."

He rose from the bed and smiled humorously at his friend.

"And now, Baron," he said, "it only remains to offer you such thanks and apologies as a lunatic may, and then clear out before the cock crows. These are my brushes, I think."

There was still something on the Baron's mind: he lay for a moment watching Mr. Bunker collect a few odds and ends and put them rapidly into a small bag, and then blurted out suddenly, "Ze Lady Alicia—do you loff her?"

"By Jove!" exclaimed Mr. Bunker, "I'd forgotten all about her. I ought to have told you that I once met her before, when she showed sympathy—practical sympathy, I may add—for an unfortunate gentleman in Clankwood. That's all."

"You do not loff her?" persisted the Baron.

"I, my dear chap? No. You are most welcome to her—*and* the countess."

"Does she not loff you?"

"On my honour, no. I told her a few early reminiscences; she happened to discover they were not what is generally known as true, and took so absurd a view of the case that I doubt whether she would speak to me again if she met me. In fact, Baron, if I read the omens aright—and I've had some experience—you only need courage and a voice."

The bed creaked, there was a volcanic upheaval of the clothes as the Baron sprang out on to the floor, and the next instant Mr. Bunker was clasped in his embrace.

"Ach, my own Bonker, forgif me! I haf suspected, I haf not been ze true friend; you have sairved me right to gom here as ze Baron. I vas too bad a Baron to gom! You have amused me, you have instrogted, you have varmed my heart. My dear frient!"

To tell the truth, Mr. Bunker looked, for the first time in their acquaintance, a little ill at ease. He laughed, but it sounded affected.

"My dear fellow—hang it! You'd make me out a martyr. As a matter of fact, I've been such a thorn as very few people would stand in their flesh. There's nothing to forgive, my dear Baron, and a lot to thank you for."

"I haf been rude, Bonker; I haf insulted you! You forgif me?"

"With all my heart, if you think it's needed, but—"

"And you vill not go now? You vill stay here?"

"What, two Barons at once? My dear chap, we'd merely confuse the butler."

"Ach, you vill joke, you hombog! But you most stay!"

"And what about my friend, Dr. Escott? No, Baron, it would only mean breakfast and the next train to Clankwood."

"Zey vill not take you ven you tell zem! I shall insist viz Sir Richard!"

"The law is the law, Baron, and I'm a certified lunatic. Here we must part till the weather clears; and mind, you mustn't say a word about my coming to see you."

The Baron looked at him disconsolately.

"You most really go, Bonker?"

"Really, Baron."

"And vere to?"

"To London town again by the milk train."

"And vat vill you do zere?"

"Look for my name."

"Bot how?"

Mr. Bunker hesitated.

"I have a little clue," he said at last, "only a thread, but I'll try it for what it's worth."

"Haf you money enoff?"

"Thanks to your generosity and my skill at billiards, yes, which reminds me that I must return poor Trelawney's ten pounds someday. At present, I can't afford to be scrupulous. So, you see, I'm provided for."

"Cigars at least, Bonker! You most smoke, my frient vizout a name!"

The Baron, night-shirted and barefooted as he was, dived into his portmanteau and produced a large box of cigars.

"You like zese, Bonker. Zey are your own choice. Smoke zem and zink of me!"

"A few, Baron, would be a pleasant reminiscence," said his friend, with a smile, "if you really insist."

"All, Bonker—I vill not keep vun! I can get more. No, you most take zem all!"

Mr. Bunker opened his bag and put in the box without a word.

"You most write," said the Baron, "tell me vere you are. I shall not tell any soul, bot ven I can, I shall gom up, and ve shall sup togezzer vunce more. Pairhaps ve may haf anozzer adventure, ha, ha!"

The Baron's laugh was almost too hearty to be true.

"I shall let you know, as soon as I find a room. It won't be in the Mayonaise this time! Good-bye: good sport and luck in love!"

"Good-bye, my frient, good-bye," said the Baron, squeezing his hand.

His friend was half out of the door when he turned, and said with an intonation quite foreign either to Beveridge or Bunker, and yet which came very pleasantly, "I forgot to warn you of one thing when I advised you to try the *rôle* of certified lunatic—you are not likely to make so good a friend as I have."

He shut the door noiselessly and was gone.

The Baron stood in the middle of the floor for fully five minutes, looking blankly at the closed door; then with a sigh he turned out the light and tumbled into bed again.

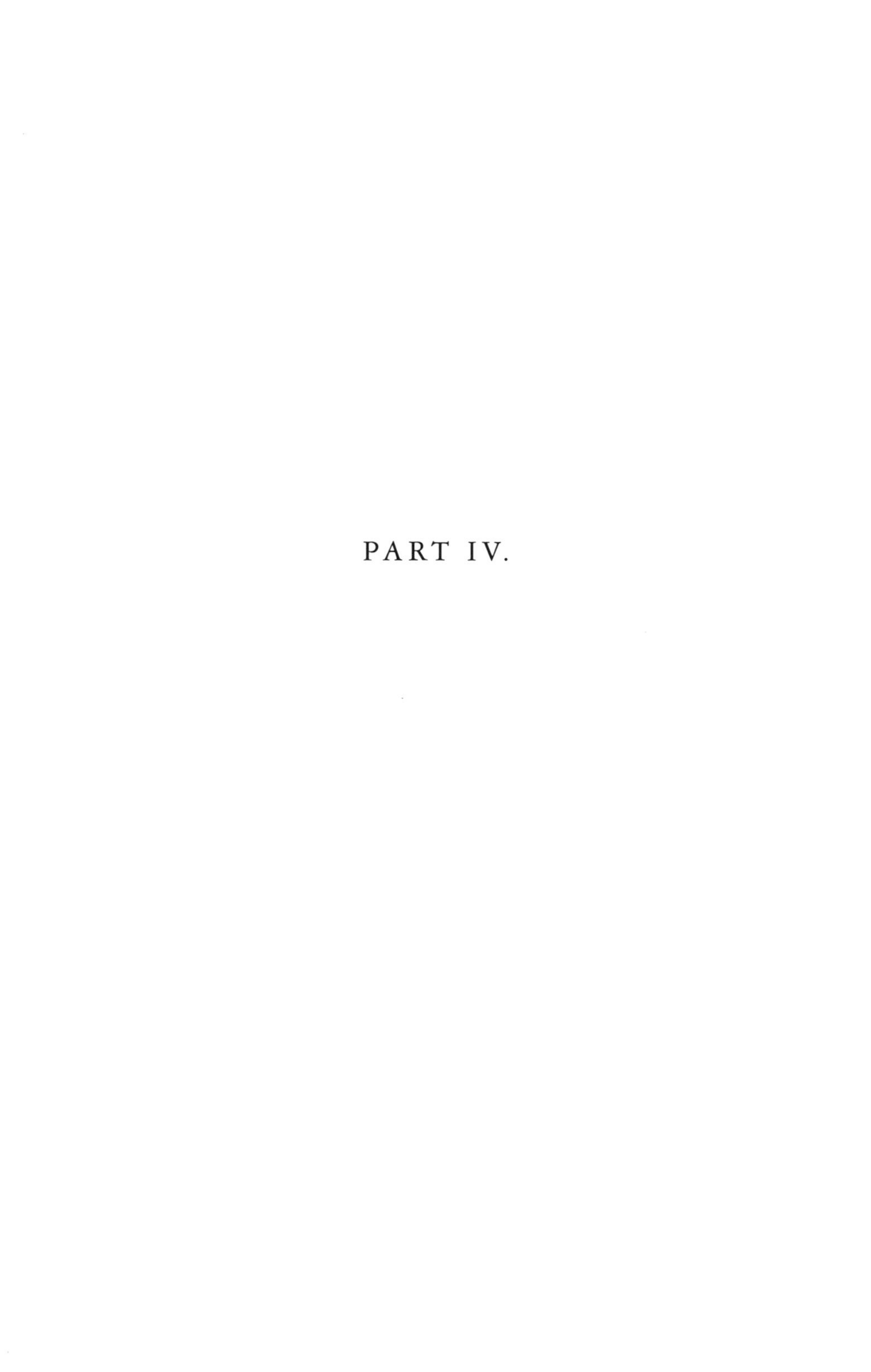

PART IV.

CHAPTER I.

The Dover express was nearing town: evening had begun to draw in, and from the wayside houses people saw the train roar by like a huge glow-worm; but they could hardly guess that it was hurrying two real actors to the climax of a real comedy.

From the opposite sides of a first-class carriage these two looked cheerfully at one another. The Channel was safely behind them, London was close ahead, and the piston of the engine seemed to thump a triumphal air.

"We've done it, Twiddel, my boy!" said the one.

"Thank Heaven!" replied the other.

"*And* myself," added his friend.

"Yes," said Twiddel; "you played your part uncommonly well, Welsh."

"It was the deuce of a fine spree!" sighed Welsh.

"The deuce," assented Twiddel.

"I'm only sorry it's all over," Welsh went on, gazing regretfully up at the lamp of the carriage. "I'd give the remains of my character and my chance of a public funeral to be starting again from Paris by the morning train!"

Twiddel laughed.

"With the same head you had that morning?"

"Yes, by George! Even with the same mile of dusty gullet!"

"It's all over now," said Twiddel, philosophically, and yet rather nervously—"at least the amusing part of it."

"All the fun, my boy, all the fun. All the dinners and the drinks, and the touching of hats to the aristocratic travellers, and the girls that sighed, and the bowing and scraping. Do you remember the sporting baronet who knew my uncle? Now, I'm plain Robert Welsh, whose uncles, as far as I am aware, don't know a baronet among 'em."

He smiled a little sardonically.

"And the baron at Fogelschloss," said Twiddel.

"Who insisted on learning my pedigree back to Alfred the Great! Gad, I gave it him, though, and I doubt whether the real Essington could have done as much. I'd rather surprise some of these noblemen if I turned up again in my true character!"

"Thank the Lord, we're not likely to meet them again!" exclaimed the doctor, devoutly.

"No," said Welsh; "here endeth the second lesson."

His friend, who had been well brought up, looked a trifle uncomfortable at this quotation.

"I say," he remarked a few minutes later, "we haven't finished yet. We've got to get the man out again, and hand him back to his friends."

"Cured," said Welsh, with a laugh.

"I wonder how he is?"

"We'll soon see."

They fell silent again, while the train hurried nearer and nearer London town. Welsh seemed to be musing on some nice point, it might be of conscience, it might also conceivably be of a more practical texture. At last he said, "There's just one thing, old man. What about the fee?"

"I'll get a cheque for it, I suppose," his friend replied, with an almost excessive air of mastery over the problem.

"Ha, ha!" laughed Welsh; "you know what I mean. It's a delicate question and all that, but, hang it, it's got to be answered."

"What has?"

"The division of the spoil."

Twiddel looked dignified.

"I'll see you get your share, old man," he answered, easily.

"But what share?"

"You suggested £100, I think."

"Out of £500 when I've done all the deceiving and told all the lies! Come, old man!"

"Well, what do you want?"

"Do you remember a certain crisis when we'd made a slip—"

"You'd made a slip!"

"*We* had made a slip, and you wanted to chuck the game and bolt? Do you remember also the terms I proposed when I offered to beard the local god almighty in his lair and explain it all away, and how he became our bosom pal and we were saved?"

"Well?"

"£300 to me, $200 to you," said Welsh, decisively.

"Rot, old man. I'll share fairly, if you insist. £250 apiece, will that do?"

Welsh said nothing, but his face was no longer the countenance of the jovial adventurer.

"It will have to, I suppose," he replied, at length.

It was with this little cloud on the horizon that they saw the lights of London twinkle through the windows, and were carried into the clamour of the platforms.

They both drove first to Twiddel's rooms; and as they looked out once more on the life and lights and traffic of the streets, their faces cleared again.

"We'll have a merry evening!" cried Welsh.

"A little supper," suggested Twiddel; "a music-hall—"

"Et cetera," added Welsh, with a laugh.

The doctor had written of their coming, and they found a fire in the back room, and the table laid.

"Ah," cried Welsh, "this looks devilish comfortable."

"A letter for me," said Twiddel; "from Billson, I think."

He read it and threw it to his friend, remarking, "I call this rather cool of him."

Welsh read—

"DEAR GEORGE—I am just off for three weeks' holiday. Sorry for leaving your practice, but I think it can look after itself till you return.

"You have only had two patients, and one fee between them. The second man vanished mysteriously. I shall tell you about it when I come back. He boned a bill, too, I fancy, but the story will keep.

"I am looking forward to hearing the true tale of your adventures. Good luck to you.—Yours ever,

"THOMAS BILLSON."

"Boned a bill?" exclaimed Welsh. "What bill, I wonder?"

"Something that came when I was away, I suppose. Hang it, I think Billson might have looked after things better!"

"It sounds queer," said Welsh, reflectively; "I wonder what it was?"

"Confound Billson, he might have told me," observed the doctor. "But, I say, you know we have something more practical to see to."

"Getting the man out again?"

"Yes."

"Well, let's have a little grub first."

Twiddel rang the bell, and the frowsy little maid entered, carrying a letter on a tray.

"Dinner," said he.

"Please, sir," began the maid, holding out the tray, "this come for you near a month agow, but Missis she bin and forgot to send it hafter you."

"Confound her!" said Twiddel, taking the letter.

He looked at the envelope, and remarked with a little start of nervous excitement, "From Dr. Congleton."

"News of Mr. Beveridge," laughed Welsh.

The doctor read the first few lines, and then, as if he had got an electric shock, the letter fell from his hand, and an expression of the most utter and lively consternation came over his face.

"Heavens!" he ejaculated, "it's all up."

"What's up?" cried Welsh, snatching at the letter.

"He's run away!"

Welsh looked at him for a moment in some astonishment, and then burst out laughing.

"What a joke!" he cried; "I don't see anything to make a fuss about. We're jolly well rid of him."

"The fee! I won't get a penny till I bring him back. And the whole thing will be found out!"

As the full meaning of this predicament burst upon Welsh, his face underwent a change by no means pleasant to watch. For a full minute he swore, and then an ominous silence fell upon the room.

Twiddel was the first to recover himself.

"Let me see the letter," he said; "I haven't finished it."

Welsh read it aloud—

"DEAR TWIDDEL—I regret to inform you that the patient, Francis Beveridge, whom you placed under my care, has escaped from Clankwood. We have made every inquiry consistent with strict privacy, but unfortunately have not yet been able to lay our hands upon him. We only know that he left Ashditch Junction in the London express, and was seen walking out of St Euston's Cross. How he has been able to maintain himself in concealment without money or clothes, I am unable to imagine.

"As no inquiries have been made for him by his cousin Mr. Welsh, or any other of his friends or relatives, I am writing to you that you may inform them, and I hope that this letter may follow you abroad without delay. I may add that the circumstances of his escape showed most unusual cunning, and could not possibly have been guarded against.

"Trusting that you are having a pleasant holiday, I am, yours very truly,

"ADOLPHUS S. CONGLETON."

The two looked at one another in silence for a minute, and then Welsh said, fiercely, "You must catch him again, Twiddel. Do you think I am going to have all my risk and trouble for nothing?"

"*I* must catch him! Do you suppose I let him loose?"

"You must catch him, all the same."

"I shan't bother my head about him," answered Twiddel, with the recklessness of despair.

"You won't? You want to have the story known, I suppose?"

"I don't care if it is."

Welsh looked at him for a minute: then he jumped up and exclaimed, "You need a drink, old man. Let's hurry up that slavey."

With the first course their countenances cleared a little, with the second they were almost composed, by the end of dinner they had started plot-hatching hopefully again.

"It's any odds on the man's still being in town," said Welsh. "He had no money or clothes, and evidently he hasn't gone to any of his friends, or the whole story would have been out. Now, there is nowhere where a man can lie low so well, especially if he is hard up, as London. I can answer from experience. He is hardly likely to be in the West End, or the best class of suburbs, so we've something to go upon at once. We must go to a private inquiry office and put men on his track, and then we must take the town in beats ourselves. So much is clear; do you see?"

"And hadn't we better find out whether anything more is known at Clankwood?" suggested Twiddel. "Dr. Congleton wrote a month ago; perhaps they have caught him by this time."

"Hardly likely, I'm afraid; he'd have written to you if they had. Still, we can but ask."

"But, I say!" the doctor suddenly exclaimed, "people may find out that I'm back without him."

Welsh was equal to the emergency.

"You must leave again at once," he said decisively, rising from the table; "and there's no good wasting time, either."

"What do you mean?" asked the bewildered doctor, who had not yet assimilated the criminal point of view.

"We'll put our luggage straight on to a cab, drive off to other rooms—I know a cheap place that will do—and if by any chance inquiries are made, people must be told that you are still abroad. Nobody must hear of your coming home tonight."

"Is it—" began Twiddel, dubiously.

"Is it what?" snapped his friend.

"Is it worth it?"

"Is £500, not to speak of two reputations, worth it! Come on!"

The unfortunate doctor sighed, and rose too. He was beginning to think that the nefarious acquisition of fees might have drawbacks after all.

CHAPTER II.

The chronicle must now go back a few days and follow another up express.

"I must either be a clergyman or a policeman," Mr. Bunker reflected, in the corner of his carriage; "they seem to me to be on the whole the two least molested professions. Each certainly has a livery which, if its occupier is ordinarily judicious, ought to serve as a certificate of sanity. To me all policemen are precisely alike, but I daresay they know them apart in the force, and as all the beats and crossings are presumably taken already, I might excite suspicion by my mere superfluity. Besides, a theatrical costumier's uniform would possibly lack some ridiculous but essential detail."

He lit another cigar and looked humorously out of the window.

"I shall take orders. An amateur theatrical clergyman's costume will be more comfortable, and probably less erroneous. They allow them some latitude, I believe; and I don't suppose there are any visible ordination scars whose absence would give me away. I shall certainly study the first reverend brother I meet to see."

Thus wisely ruminating, he arrived in London at a very early hour on a chilly morning, and drove straight to a small hotel near King's Cross, where the landlord was much gratified at receiving so respectable a guest as the Rev. Alexander Butler. ("I must begin with a B." said Mr. Bunker to himself; "I think it's lucky.")

It is true the reverend gentleman was in evening clothes, while his hat and coat had a singularly secular, not to say fashionable, appearance; but, as he mentioned casually in the course of some extremely affable remarks, he had been dining in a country house, and had not thought it worth while changing before he left. After breakfasting he dressed himself in an equally secular suit of tweeds and went out, he mentioned incidentally, to call at his tailor's for his professional habit, which he seemed surprised to learn had not yet been forwarded to the hotel.

A visit to a certain well-known firm of theatrical costumiers was followed by his reappearance in a cab accompanied by a bulky brown paper parcel; and presently he emerged from his room attired more consistently with his office, much to his own satisfaction, for, as he observed, "I cannot say I approve of clergymen masquerading as laymen."

His opinion on the converse circumstance was not expressed.

Much to his landlord's disappointment, he informed him that he should probably leave again that afternoon, and then he went out for a walk.

About half an hour later he was once more in the street where, not so very long ago, a very exciting cab-race had finished. He strolled slowly past Dr. Twiddel's house. The blinds of the front room were down; at that hour there was no sign of life about it, and he saw nothing at all to arrest his attention. Then he looked down the other side of the street, and to his great satisfaction spied a card, with the legend "Apartments to let," in one of the first-floor windows of a house immediately opposite.

He rang the bell, and in a moment a rotund and loquacious landlady appeared. Yes, the drawing-room was to let; would the reverend gentleman come up and see it? Mr. Bunker went up, and approved. They readily agreed upon terms, and the landlady, charmed with her new lodger's appearance and manners, no less than with the respectability of his profession, proceeded to descant at some length on the quiet, comfort, and numerous other advantages of the apartments.

"Just the very plice you wants, sir. We 'ave 'ad clerical gentlemen 'ere before, sir; in fact, there's one a-staying 'ere now, second floor—you may know of 'im, sir—the Reverend Mr. John Duggs; a very pleasant gentleman you'll find him, sir. I'll tell 'im you're 'ere, sir; 'e'd be sure to like to meet another gentleman of the syme cloth, has they say."

Somehow or other the Rev. Mr. Butler failed to display the hearty pleasure at this announcement that the worthy Mrs. Gabbon had naturally expected.

Aloud he merely said, "Indeed," politely, but with no unusual interest.

Within himself he reflected, "The deuce take Mr. John Duggs! However, I want the rooms, and a man must risk something."

As a precautionary measure he visited a second-hand bookseller on his way back, and purchased a small assortment of the severest-looking works on theology they kept in stock; and these, with his slender luggage, he brought round to Mrs. Gabbon's in the course of the afternoon.

He looked carefully out of his sitting-room window, but the doctor's blinds were still down, and he saw no one coming or going about the house; so he began his inquiries by calling up his landlady.

"I have been troubled with lumbago, Mrs. Gabbon," he began.

"Dearie me, sir," said Mrs. Gabbon, "I'm sorry to 'ear that; you that looks so 'ealthy too! Well, one never knows what's be'ind a 'appy hexterior, does one, sir?"

"No, Mrs. Gabbon," replied Mr. Bunker, solemnly; "one never knows what even a clergyman's coat conceals."

"That's very true, sir. In the midst of life we are in—"

"Lumbago," interposed Mr. Bunker.

Mrs. Gabbon looked a trifle startled.

"Well," he continued with the same gravity, "I may unfortunately have occasion to consult a doctor—"

"There's Dr. Smith," interrupted Mrs. Gabbon, her equanimity quite restored by his ecclesiastical tone and the mention of ailments; " 'e attended my poor dear 'usband hall through his last illness; an huncommon clever doctor, sir, as I ought to know, sir, bein'—"

"No doubt an excellent man, Mrs. Gabbon; but I should like to know of one as near at hand as possible. Now I see the name of a Dr. Twiddel—"

"I wouldn't recommend 'im, sir," said Mrs. Gabbon, pursing her mouth.

"Indeed? Why not?"

" 'E attended Mrs. Brown's servant-girl, sir—she bein' the lady as has the 'ouse next door—and what he give 'er didn't do no good. Mrs. Brown tell me 'erself."

"Still, in an emergency—"

"Besides which, he ain't at 'ome, sir."

"Where has he gone?"

"Abroad, they do say, sir; though I don't rightly know much about 'im."

"Has he been away long?"

Mrs. Gabbon considered.

"It must 'ave bin before the middle of November he went, sir."

"Ha!" exclaimed Mr. Bunker, keenly, though apparently more to himself than his landlady.

"I beg your pardon, sir?"

"The middle of November, you say? That's a long holiday for a doctor to take."

" 'E 'avn't no practice to speak of—not as I knows of, leastways."

"What sort of a man is he—young or old?"

"By my opinion, sir, 'e's too young. I don't 'old by them young doctors. Now Dr. Smith, sir—"

"Dr. Twiddel is quite a young man, then?"

"What I'd call little better than a boy, sir. They tell me they lets 'em loose very young nowadays."

"About twenty-five, say?"

" 'E might be that, sir; but I don't know much about 'im, sir. Now Dr. Smith, sir, 'e's different."

In fact at this point Mrs. Gabbon showed such a tendency to turn the conversation back to the merits of Dr. Smith and the precise nature of Mr. Bunker's ailment, that her lodger, in despair, requested her to bring up a cup of tea as speedily as possible.

"Before the middle of November," he said to himself. "It is certainly a curious coincidence."

To a gentleman of Mr. Bunker's sociable habits and active mind, the prospect of sitting day by day in the company of his theological treatises and talkative landlady, and watching an apparently uninhabited house, seemed at first sight even less entertaining than a return to Clankwood. But, as he said of himself, he possessed a kind of easy workaday philosophy, and, besides that, an apparently irresistible attraction for the incidents of life.

He had barely finished his cup of tea, and was sitting over the fire smoking one of the Baron's cigars and looking through one of the few books he had brought that bore no relation to divinity, his feet high upon the side of the mantelpiece, his ready-made costume perhaps a little more unbuttoned than the strictest propriety might approve, and a stiff glass of whisky-and-water at his elbow, when there came a rap at his door.

In response to his "Come in," a middle-aged gentleman, dressed in clerical attire, entered. He had a broad, bearded face, a dull eye, and an indescribably average aspect.

"The devil! Mr. John Duggs himself," thought Mr. Bunker, hastily adopting a more conventional attitude and feeling for his button-holes.

"Ah—er—Mr. Butler, I believe?" said the stranger, with an apologetic air.

"The same," replied Mr. Bunker, smiling affably.

"I," continued his visitor, advancing with more confidence, "am Mr. Duggs. I am dwelling at present in the apartment immediately above you, and hearing of the arrival of a fellow-clergyman, through my worthy friend Mrs. Gabbon, I have taken the liberty of calling. She gave me to understand that you were not undesirous of making my acquaintance, Mr. Butler."

"The deuce, she did!" thought Mr. Butler. Aloud he answered most politely, "I am honoured, Mr. Duggs. Won't you sit down?"

First casting a wary eye upon a chair, Mr. Duggs seated himself carefully on the edge of it.

"It is quite evident," thought Mr. Bunker, "that he has spotted something wrong. I believe a bobby would have been safer after all."

He assumed the longest face he could draw, and remarked sententiously, "The weather has been unpleasantly cold of late, Mr. Duggs."

He flattered himself that his guest seemed instantly more at his ease. Certainly he replied with as much cordiality as a man with such a dull eye could be supposed to display.

"It has, Mr. Butler; in fact I have suffered from a chill for some weeks. Ahem!"

"Have something to drink," suggested Mr. Bunker, sympathetically. "I'm trying a little whisky myself, as a cure for cold."

"I—ah—I am sorry. I do not touch spirits."

"I, on the contrary, am glad to hear it. Too few of our clergymen nowadays support the cause of temperance by example."

Mr. Bunker felt a little natural pride in this happily expressed sentiment, but his visitor merely turned his cold eye on the whisky bottle, and breathed heavily.

"Confound him!" he thought; "I'll give him something to snort at if he is going to conduct himself like this."

"Have a cigar?" he asked aloud.

Mr. Duggs seemed to regard the cigar-box a little less unkindly than the whisky bottle; but after a careful look at it he replied, "I am afraid they seem a little too strong for me. I am a light smoker, Mr. Butler."

"Really," smiled Mr. Bunker; "so many virtues in one room reminds me of the virgins of Gomorrah."

"I beg your pardon? The what?" asked Mr. Duggs, with a startled stare.

Mr. Bunker suspected that he had made a slip in his biblical reminiscences, but he continued to smile imperturbably, and inquired with a perfect air of surprise, "Haven't you read the novel I referred to?"

Mr. Duggs appeared a little relieved, but he answered blankly enough, "I—ah—have not. What is the book you refer to?"

"Oh, don't you know? To tell the truth, I forget the title. It's by a somewhat well-known lady writer of religious fiction. A Miss—her name escapes me at this moment."

In fact, as Mr. Bunker had no idea how long his friend might be dwelling in the apartment immediately above him, he thought it more prudent to make no statement that could possibly be checked.

"I am no great admirer of religious fiction of any kind," replied Mr. Duggs, "particularly that written by emotional females."

"No," said Mr. Bunker, pleasantly; "I should imagine your own doctrines were not apt to err on the sentimental side."

"I am not aware that I have said anything to you about my—doctrines, as you call them, Mr. Butler."

"Still, don't you think one can generally tell a man's creed from his coat, and his sympathies from the way he cocks his hat?"

"I think," replied Mr. Duggs, "that our ideas of our vocation are somewhat different."

"Mine is, I admit," said Mr. Bunker, who had come to the conclusion that the strain of playing his part was really too great, and was now being happily carried along by his tongue.

Mr. Duggs for a moment was evidently disposed to give battle, but thinking better of it, he contented himself with frowning at his younger opponent, and abruptly changed the subject.

"May I ask what position you hold in the church, Mr. Butler?"

"Why," began Mr. Bunker, lightly: it was on the tip of his tongue to say "a clergyman, of course," when he suddenly recollected that he might be anything from the rank of curate up to the people who wear gaiters (and who these were precisely he didn't know). An ingenious solution suggested itself. He replied with a preliminary inquiry, "Have you ever been in the East, Mr. Duggs?"

"I regret to say I have not hitherto had the opportunity."

"Thank the Lord for that," thought Mr. Bunker. "I have been a missionary," he said quietly, and looked dreamily into the fire.

It was a happy move. Mr. Duggs was visibly impressed.

"Ah?" he said. "Indeed? I am much interested to learn this, Mr. Butler. It—ah—gives me perhaps a somewhat different view of your—ah—opinions. Where did your work lie?"

"China," replied Mr. Bunker, thinking it best to keep as far abroad as possible.

"Ha!" exclaimed Mr. Duggs. "This is really extremely fortunate. I am at present, Mr. Butler, studying the religions and customs of China at the British Museum, with a view to going out there myself very shortly. I already feel I know almost as much about that most interesting country as if I had lived there. I should like to talk with you at some length on the subject."

Mr. Bunker saw that it was time to put an end to this conversation, at whatever minor risk of perturbing his visitor. He had been a little alarmed, too, by noticing that Mr. Duggs's dull eye had wandered frequently to his theological library, which with his usual foresight he had strewn conspicuously on the table, and that any expression it had was rather of suspicious curiosity than gratification.

"I should like to hear some of your experiences," Mr. Duggs continued. "In what province did you work?"

"In Hung Hang Ho," replied Mr. Bunker. His visitor looked puzzled, but he continued boldly, "My experiences were somewhat unpleasant. I became engaged to a mandarin's daughter—a charming girl. I was suspected, however, of abetting an illicit traffic in Chinese lanterns. My companions were manicured alive, and I only made my escape in a pagoda, or a junk—I was in too much of a hurry to notice which—at the imminent peril of my life. Don't go to China, Mr. Duggs."

Mr. Duggs rose.

"Young man," he said, sternly, "put away that fatal bottle. I can only suppose that it is under the influence of drink that you have ventured to tell me such an irreverent and impossible story."

"Sir," began Mr. Bunker, warmly—for he thought that an outburst of indignation would probably be the safest way of concluding the interview—when he stopped abruptly and listened. All the time his ears had been alive to anything going on outside, and now he heard a cab rattle up and stop close by. It might be at Dr. Twiddel's he thought, and, turning from his visitor, he sprang to the window.

Remarking distantly, "I hear a cab; it is possibly a friend I am expecting," Mr. Duggs stepped to the other window.

It was only, however, a hansom at the door of the next house, out of which a very golden-haired young lady was stepping.

"Aha," said Mr. Bunker, quite forgetting the indignant *rôle* he had begun to play; "rather nice! Is this your friend, Mr. Duggs?"

Mr. Duggs gave him one look of his dull eyes, and walked straight for the door. As he went out he merely remarked, "Our acquaintance has been brief, Mr. Butler, but it has been quite sufficient."

"Quite," thought Mr. Bunker.

CHAPTER III.

That was Mr. Bunker's first and last meeting with the Rev. John Duggs, and he took no small credit to himself for having so effectually incensed his neighbour, without, at the same time, bringing suspicion on anything more pertinent than his sobriety.

And yet sometimes in the course of the next three days he would have been thankful to see him again, if only to have another passage-of-arms. The time passed most wearily; the consulting-room blinds were never raised; no cabs stopped before the doctor's door; nobody except the little servant ever moved about the house.

He could think of no plan better than waiting; and so he waited, showing himself seldom in the streets, and even sitting behind the curtain while he watched at the window. After writing at some length to the Baron he had no further correspondence that he could distract himself with; he was even forced once or twice to dip into the theological works. Mrs. Gabbon had evidently " 'eard sommat" from Mr. Duggs, and treated him to little of her society. The boredom became so excessive that he decided he must make a move soon, however rash it was.

The only active step he took, and indeed the only step he saw his way to take, was a call on Dr. Twiddel's *locum.* But luck seemed to run dead against him. Dr. Billson had departed "on his holiday," he was informed, and would not return for three weeks. So Mr. Bunker was driven back to his window and the Baron's cigars.

It was the evening of his fourth day in Mrs. Gabbon's rooms. He had finished a modest dinner and was dealing himself hands at piquet with an old pack of cards, when he heard the rattle of a cab coming up the street. The usual faint flicker of hope rose: the cab stopped below him, the flicker burned brighter, and in an instant he was at the window. He opened the slats of the blind, and the flicker was aflame. Before the doctor's house a four-wheeled cab was standing laden with luggage, and two men were going up the steps. He watched the luggage being taken in and the cab drive away, and then he turned radiantly back to the fire.

"The curtain is up," he said to himself. "What's the first act to be?"

Presently he put on his wideawake hat and went out for a stroll. He walked slowly past the doctor's house, but there was nothing to be seen or heard. Remembering the room at the back, he was not surprised to find no chink of light about the front windows, and thinking it better not to run the risk of being seen lingering there, he walked on.

He was in such good spirits, and had been cooped up so continually for the last few days, that he went on and on, and it was not till about a couple of hours had passed that he approached his rooms again. As he came down the street he was surprised to see by the light of a lamp that another four-wheeler was standing before the doctor's house, also laden with luggage.

Two men jumped in, one after another, and when he had come at his fastest walk within twenty yards or so, the cabman whipped up and drove rapidly away, luggage and men and all.

He looked up and down for a hansom, but there were none to be seen. For a few yards he set off at a run in pursuit, and then, finding that the horse was being driven at a great rate, and remembering the paucity of stray cabs in the quiet streets and roads round about, he stopped and considered the question.

"After all," he reflected, "it may not have been Dr. Twiddel who drove away; in fact, if it was he who arrived in the first cab, it's any odds against it. Pooh! It can't be. Still, it's a curious thing if two cabs loaded with luggage came to the house in the same evening, and one drove away without unlading."

With his spirits a little damped in spite of his philosophy, he went back to his rooms.

In the morning the consulting-room blinds were still down, and the house looked as deserted as ever.

He waited till lunch, and then he went out boldly and pulled the doctor's bell. The same little maid appeared, but she evidently did not recognise the fashionable patient who disappeared so mysteriously in the demure-looking clergyman at the door.

"Is Dr. Twiddel at home?"

"No, sir, he ain't back yet."

"He hasn't been back?"

"No, sir."

Mr. Bunker looked at her keenly, and then said to himself, "She is lying."

He thought he would try a chance shot.

"But he was expected home last night, I believe."

The maid looked a little staggered.

"He ain't been," she replied.

"I happen to have heard that he called here," he hazarded again.

This time she was evidently put about.

"He ain't been here—as I knows of."

He slipped half-a-crown into her hand.

"Think again," he said, in his most winning accents.

The poor little maid was obviously in a dilemma.

"Do you want him particular, sir?"

"Particularly."

She fidgeted a little.

"He told me," he pursued, "that he might look in at his rooms last night. He left no message for me?"

"What nime, sir?"

"Mr. Butler."

"No, sir."

"Then, my dear," said Mr. Bunker, with his most insinuating smile, "he was here for a little, you can't deny?"

At the maid's embarrassed glance down his long coat, he suddenly realised that there was perhaps a distinction between lay and clerical smiles.

"He might have just looked in, sir," she admitted.

"But he didn't want it known?"

"No, sir."

"Quite right, I advised him not to, and you did very well not to tell me at first."

He smiled approvingly and made a pretence of turning away.

"Oh, by the way," he added, stopping as if struck by an afterthought, "Is he still in town? He promised to leave word for me, but he has evidently forgotten."

"I don't know, sir; 'e didn't say."

"What? He left *no* word at all?"

"No, sir."

Mr. Bunker held out another half-crown.

"It's truth, sir," said the maid, drawing back; "we don't know where 'e is."

"Take it, all the same; you have been very discreet. You have no idea?"

The maid hesitated.

"I *did* 'ear Mr. Welsh say something about lookin' for rooms," she allowed.

"In London?"

"I expect so, sir; but 'e didn't say no more."

"Mr. Welsh is the friend who came with him, of course?"

"Yes, sir."

"Thanks," said Mr. Bunker. "By the way, Dr. Twiddel might not like your telling this even to a friend, so you needn't say I called, I'll tell him myself when I see him, and I won't give you away."

He smiled benignly, and the little maid thanked him quite gratefully.

"Evidently," he thought as he went away, "I was meant for something in the detective line."

He returned to his rooms to meditate, and the longer he thought the more puzzled he became, and yet the more convinced that he had taken up a thread that must lead him somewhere.

"As for my plan of action," he considered, "I see nothing better for it than staying where I am—and watching. This mysterious doctor must surely steal back some night. Now and then I might go round the town and try a cast in the likeliest bars—oh, hang me, though! I forgot I was a clergyman."

That night he had a welcome distraction in the shape of a letter from the Baron. It was written from Brierley Park, in the Baron's best pointed German hand, and it ran thus—

"MY DEAR BUNKER— I was greatly more delighted than I am able to express to you from the amusing correspondence you addressed me. How glad I am, I can assure you, that you are still in safety and comfort. Remember, my dear friend, to call for me when need arises, although I do think you can guard yourself as well as most alone.

"This leaves me happy and healthful, and in utmost prosperity with the kind Sir Richard and his charming Lady. You English certainly know well how to cause time to pass with mirth. About instruction I say less!

"They have talked of you here. I laugh and keep my tongue when they wonder who he is and whither gone away. Now that anger is passed and they see I myself enjoy the joke, they say, and especially do the ladies, (You humbug, Bunker!) 'How charming was the imitation, Baron!' You can indeed win the hearts, if wishful so. The Lady Grillyer and her unexpressable daughter I have often seen. Today they come here for two nights. I did suggest it to Lady Brierley, and I fear she did suspect the condition of my heart; but she charmingly smiled, she asked them, and they come!

"The Countess, I fear, does not now love you much, my friend; but then she knows not the truth. The Lady Alicia is strangely silent on the matter of Mr. Bunker, but in time she also doubtless will forgive." (At this Mr. Bunker smiled in some amusement.)

"When they leave Brierley I also shall take my departure on the following day, that is in three days. Therefore write hastily, Bunker, and name the place and hour where we shall meet again and dine festively. I expect a most reverent clergyman and much instructive discourse. Ah, humbug!—Thine always,

"RUDOLPH VON BLITZENBERG.

"*P.S.*—She is sometimes more kind and sometimes so distant. Ah, I know not what to surmise! But tomorrow or the next my fate will be decided. Give me of your prayers, my reverent friend, R. VON B."

"Dear old Baron!" said Mr. Bunker. "Well, I've at least a dinner to look forward to."

CHAPTER IV.

Dr. Twiddel, meanwhile, was no less anxious to make the Rev. Alexander Butler's acquaintance than the Rev. Alexander Butler was to make his. Not that he was aware of that gentleman's recent change of identity and occupation; but most industrious endeavors to find a certain Mr. Beveridge were made in the course of the next few days. He and Welsh were living modestly and obscurely in the neighbourhood of Pentonville Road, scouring the town by day, studying a map and laying the most ingenious plans at night. Welsh's first effort, as soon as they were established in their new quarters, was to induce his friend to go down to Clankwood and make further inquiries, but this Twiddel absolutely declined to do.

"My dear chap," he answered, "supposing anything were found out, or even suspected, what am I to say? Old Congleton knows me well, and for his own sake doesn't want to make a fuss; but if he really spots that something is wrong, he will be so afraid of his reputation that he'd give me away like a shot."

"How are you going to give things away by going down and seeing him?"

"*If* they have guessed anything, I'll give it away. I haven't your cheek, you know, and tact, and that sort of thing; you'd much better go yourself."

"*I*? It isn't my business."

"You seem to be making it yours. Besides, Dr. Congleton thinks it is. You passed yourself off as the chap's cousin, and it is quite natural for you to go and inquire."

Welsh pondered the point. "Hang it," he said at last, "it would do just as well to write. Perhaps it's safer after all."

"Well, you write."

"Why should I, rather than you?"

"Because you're his cousin."

Welsh considered again. "Well, I don't suppose it matters much. I'll write, if you're afraid."

It was these amiable little touches in his friend's conversation that helped to make Twiddel's lot at this time so pleasant. In fact, the doctor was learning a good deal about human nature in cloudy weather.

With great care Welsh composed a polite note of anxious inquiry, and by return of post received the following reply—

"MY DEAR SIR—I regret to inform you that we have not so far recovered your cousin Mr. Beveridge. In all probability, however, this cannot be long delayed now, as he was seen within the last week at a country house in Dampshire, and is known to have fled to London immediately on his recognition, but before he could be secured. He was then clean shaved, and had been passing under the name of Francis Bunker. We are making strict inquiries for him in London.

"Nobody can regret the unfortunate circumstance of his escape more than I, and, in justice to myself and my institution, I can assure you that it was only through the most unforeseen and remarkable ingenuity on your cousin's part that it occurred.

"Trusting that I may soon be able to inform you of his recovery, I am, yours very truly,

"ADOLPHUS S. CONGLETON."

Their ardour was, if possible, increased by Dr. Congleton's letter.

Mr. Beveridge was almost certainly in London, and they knew now that they must look for a clean-shaved man. Two private inquiry detectives were at work; and on their own account they had mapped the likeliest parts of London into beats, visiting every bar and restaurant in turn, and occasionally hanging about stations and the stopping-places for 'buses.

It was dreadfully hard work, and after four days of it, even Welsh began to get a little sickened.

"Hang it," he said in the evening, "I haven't had a decent dinner since we came back. Mr. Bunker can go to the devil for tonight, I'm going to dine decently. I'm sick of going round pubs, and not even stopping to have a drink."

"So am I," replied Twiddel, cordially; "where shall we go?"

"The Café Maccarroni," suggested Welsh; "we can't afford a West-end place, and they give one a very decent dinner there."

The Café Maccarroni in Holborn is nominally of foreign extraction—certainly the waiters and the stout proprietor come from sunnier lands—and many of the diners you can hear talking in strange tongues, with quick gesticulations. But for the most part they are respectable citizens of London, who drink Chianti because it stimulates cheaply and not unpleasantly. The white-painted room is bright and clean and seldom very crowded, the British palate can be tickled with tolerable joints and cutlets, and the foreign with gravy-covered odds and ends. Altogether, it may be recommended to such as desire to dine comfortably and not too conspicuously.

The hour at which the two friends entered was later than most of the *habitués* dine, and they had the room almost to themselves. They faced each other across a small table beside the wall, and very soon the discomforts of their researches began to seem more tolerable.

"We'll catch him soon, old man," said Welsh, smiling more affably than he had smiled since they came back. "A day or two more of this kind of work and even London won't be able to conceal him any longer."

"Dash it, we must," replied Twiddel, bravely. "We'll show old Congleton how to look for a lunatic."

"Ha, ha!" laughed Welsh, "I think he'll be rather relieved himself. Waiter! Another bottle of the same."

The bottle arrived, and the waiter was just filling their glasses when a young clergyman entered the room and walked quietly towards the farther end. Welsh raised his glass and exclaimed, "Here's luck to ourselves, Twiddel, old man!"

At that moment the clergyman was passing their table, and at the mention of this toast he started almost imperceptibly, and then, throwing a quick glance at the two, stopped and took a seat at the next table, with his back turned towards them. Welsh, who was at the farther side, looked at him with some annoyance, and made a sign to Twiddel to talk a little more quietly.

To the waiter, who came with the menu, the clergyman explained in a quiet voice that he was waiting for a friend, and asked for an evening paper instead, in which he soon appeared to be deeply engrossed.

At first the conversation went on in a lower tone, but in a few minutes they insensibly forgot their neighbour, and the voices rose again by starts.

"My dear fellow," Welsh was saying, "we can discuss that afterwards; we haven't caught him yet."

"I want to settle it now."

"But I thought it was settled."

"No, it wasn't," said Twiddel, with a foreign and vinous doggedness.

"What do you suggest then?"

"Divide it equally—£250 each."

"You think you can claim half the credit for the idea and half the trouble?"

"I can claim *all* the risk—practically."

"Pooh!" said Welsh. "You think I risked nothing? Come, come, let's talk of something else."

"Oh, rot!" interrupted Twiddel, who by this time was decidedly flushed. "You needn't ride the high horse like that, you are not Mr. Mandell-Essington any longer."

With a violent start, the clergyman brought his fist crash on the table, and exclaimed aloud, "By Heaven, that's it!"

CHAPTER V.

As one may suppose, everybody in the room started in great astonishment at this extraordinary outburst. With a sharp "Hollo!" Twiddel turned in his seat, to see the clergyman standing over him with a look of the keenest inquiry in his well-favoured face.

"May I ask, Dr. Twiddel, what you know of the gentleman you just named?" he said, with perfect politeness.

The conscience-smitten doctor gazed at him blankly, and the colour suddenly left his face. But Welsh's nerves were stronger; and, as he looked hard at the stranger, a jubilant light leaped to his eyes.

"It's our man!" he cried, before his friend could gather his wits. "It's Beveridge, or Bunker, or whatever he calls himself! Waiter!"

Instantly three waiters, all agog, hurried at his summons.

Mr. Bunker regarded him with considerable surprise. He had quite expected that the pair would be thrown into confusion, but not that it would take this form.

"Excuse me, sir," he began, but Welsh interrupted him by crying to the leading waiter—

"Fetch a four-wheeled cab and a policeman, quick!" As the man hesitated, he added, "This man here is an escaped lunatic."

The waiter was starting for the door, when Mr. Bunker stepped out quickly and interrupted him.

"Stop one minute, waiter," he said, with a quiet, unruffled air that went far to establish his sanity. "Do I look like a lunatic? Kindly call the proprietor first."

The stout proprietor was already on his way to their table, and the one or two other diners were beginning to gather round. Mr. Bunker's manner had impressed even Welsh, and after his nature he took refuge in bluster.

"I say, my man," he cried, "this won't pass. Somebody fetch a cab."

"Vat is dees about?" asked the proprietor, coming up.

"Your wine, I'm afraid, has been rather too powerful for this gentleman," Mr. Bunker explained, with a smile.

"Look here," blustered Welsh, "do you know you've got a lunatic in the room?"

"You can perhaps guess it," smiled Mr. Bunker, indicating Welsh with his eyes.

The waiters began to twitter, and Welsh, with an effort, pulled himself together.

"My friend here," he said, "is Dr. Twiddel, a well-known practitioner in London. He can tell you that he certified this man as a lunatic, and that he afterwards escaped from his asylum. That is so, Twiddel?"

"Yes," assented Twiddel, whose colour was beginning to come back a little.

"Who are you, sare?" asked the proprietor.

"Show him your card, Twiddel," said Welsh, producing his own and handing it over.

The proprietor looked at both cards, and then turned to Mr. Bunker.

"And who are you, sare?"

"My name is Mandell-Essington."

"His name—" began Welsh.

"Have you a card?" interposed the proprietor.

"I am sorry I have not," replied Mr. Bunker (to still call him by the name of his choice).

"His name is Francis Beveridge," said Welsh.

"I beg your pardon; it is Mandell-Essington."

"Any other description?" Welsh asked, with a sneer.

"A gentleman, I believe."

"No other occupation?"

"Not unless you can call a justice of the peace such," replied Mr. Bunker, with a smile.

"And yet he disguises himself as a clergyman!" exclaimed Welsh, triumphantly, turning to the proprietor.

Mr. Bunker saw that he was caught, but he merely laughed, and observed, "My friend here disguises himself in liquor, a much less respectable cloak."

Unfortunately the humour of this remark was somewhat thrown away on his present audience; indeed, coming from a professed clergyman, it produced an unfavourable impression.

"You are not a clergyman?" said the proprietor, suspiciously.

"I am glad to say I am not," replied Mr. Bunker, frankly.

"Den vat do you do in dis dress?"

"I put it on as a compliment to the cloth; I retain it at present for decency," said Mr. Bunker, whose tongue had now got a fair start of him.

"Mad," remarked Welsh, confidentially, shrugging his shoulders with really excellent dramatic effect.

By this time the audience were disposed to agree with him.

"You can give no better account of yourself dan dis?" asked the proprietor.

"I am anxious to," replied Mr. Bunker, "but a public restaurant is not the place in which I choose to give it."

"Fetch the cab and the policeman," said Welsh to a waiter.

At this moment another gentleman entered the room, and at the sight of him Mr. Bunker's face brightened, and he stopped the waiter by a cry of, "Wait one moment; here comes a gentleman who knows me."

Everybody turned, and beheld a burly, very fashionably dressed young man, with a fair moustache and a cheerful countenance.

"Ach, Bonker!" he cried.

This confirmation of Mr. Bunker's *aliases* ought, one would expect, to have delighted the two conspirators, but, instead, it produced the most remarkable effect. Twiddel utterly collapsed, while even Welsh's impudence at last deserted him. Neither said a word as the Baron von Blitzenberg greeted his friend with affectionate heartiness.

"My friend, zis is good for ze heart! Bot, how? Vat makes it here?"

"My dear Baron, the most unfortunate mistake has occurred. Two men here—" But at this moment he stopped in great surprise, for the Baron was staring hard first at Welsh and then at Twiddel.

"Ah!" he exclaimed, "Mr. Mandell-Essington, I zink?"

Welsh hesitated for an instant, and his hesitation was evident to all. Then he replied, "No, you are mistaken."

"Surely I cannot be; you did stay in Fogelschloss?" said the Baron. "Is not zis Dr. Twiddel?"

"No—er—ah—yes," stammered Twiddel, looking feebly at Welsh.

The Baron looked from the one to the other in great perplexity, when Mr. Bunker, who had been much puzzled by this conversation, broke in, "Did you call that person Mandell-Essington?"

"I cairtainly zought it vas."

"Where did you meet him?"

"In Bavaria, at my own castle."

"You are mistaken, sir," said Welsh.

"One moment, Mr. Welsh," said Mr. Bunker. "How long ago was this, Baron?"

"Jost before I gom to London. He travelled viz zis ozzer gentleman, Dr. Twiddel."

"You are wrong, sir," persisted Welsh.

"For his health," added the Baron.

A light began to dawn on Mr. Bunker.

"His health?" he cried, and then smiled politely at Welsh. "We will talk this over, Mr. Welsh."

"I am sorry I happen to be going," said Welsh, taking his hat and coat.

"What, without your lunatic?" asked Mr. Bunker.

"That is Dr. Twiddel's affair, not mine. Kindly let me pass, sir."

"No, Mr. Welsh; if you go now, it will be in the company of that policeman you were so anxious to send for." There was such an unmistakable threat in Mr. Bunker's voice and eye that Welsh hesitated. "We will talk it over, Mr. Welsh," Mr. Bunker repeated distinctly. "Kindly sit down. I have several things to ask you and your friend Dr. Twiddel."

Muttering something under his breath, Welsh hung up his coat and hat, sat down, and then assuming an air of great impudence, remarked, "Fire away, Mr. Mandell-Essington—Beveridge—Bunker, or whatever you call yourself."

Without paying the slightest attention to this piece of humour, Mr. Bunker turned to the bewildered proprietor, and, to the intense disappointment of the audience, said, "You can leave us now, thank you; our talk is likely to be of a somewhat private nature." As their gallery withdrew, he drew up a chair for the Baron, and all four sat round the small table.

"Now," said Mr. Bunker to Welsh, "you will perhaps be kind enough to give me a precise account of your doings since the middle of November."

"I'm d—d if I do," replied Welsh.

"Sare," interposed the Baron in his stateliest manner, "I know not now who you may be, but I see you are no gentleman. Ven you are viz gentlemen—and noblemen—you vill please to speak respectfully."

The stare that Welsh attempted in reply was somewhat ineffective.

"Perhaps, Dr. Twiddel, you can give the account I want?" said Mr. Bunker.

The poor doctor looked at his friend, hesitated, and finally stammered out, "I—I don't see why."

Mr. Bunker pulled a paper out of his pocket and showed it to him.

"Perhaps this may suggest a why."

When the doctor saw the bill for Mr. Beveridge's linen, the last of his courage ebbed away. He glanced helplessly at Welsh, but his ally was now leaning back in his chair with such an irritating assumption of indifference, and the prospective fee had so obviously vanished, that he was suddenly seized with the most virtuous resolutions.

"What do you want to know, sir?" he asked.

"In the first place, how did you come to have anything to do with me?"

Welsh, whose sharp wits instantly divined the weak point in the attack, cut in quickly, "Don't tell him if he doesn't know already!"

But Twiddel's relapse to virtue was complete. "I was asked to take charge of you while—" He hesitated.

"While I was unwell," smiled Mr. Bunker. "Yes?"

"I was to travel with you."

"Ah!"

"But I—I didn't like the idea, you see; and so—in fact—Welsh suggested that I should take him instead."

"While you locked me up in Clankwood?"

"Yes."

"Ha, ha, ha!" laughed Mr. Bunker, "I must say it was a devilish humorous idea."

At this Twiddel began to take heart again.

"I am very sorry, sir, for—" he began, when the Baron interrupted excitedly.

"Zen vat is your name, Bonker?"

"*I* am Mr. Mandell-Essington, Baron."

The Baron looked at the other two in turn with wide-open eyes. Then he turned indignantly upon Welsh.

"You were impostor zen, sare? You gom to my house and call yourself a gentleman, and impose upon me, and tell of your family and your estates. You, a low—er—er—vat you say?—a low *cad!* Bonker, I cannot sit at ze same table viz zese persons!"

He rose as he spoke.

"One moment, Baron! Before we send these gentlemen back to their really promising career of fraud, I want to ask one or two more questions." He turned to Twiddel. "What were you to be paid for this?"

"£500."

Mr. Bunker opened his eyes. "That's the way my money goes? From your anxiety to recapture me, I presume you have not yet been paid?"

"No, I assure you, Mr. Essington," said Twiddel, eagerly; "I give you my word."

"I shall judge by the circumstances rather than your word, sir. It is perhaps unnecessary to inform you that you have had your trouble for nothing." He looked at them both as though they were curious animals, and then continued: "You, Mr. Welsh, are a really wonderfully typical rascal. I am glad to have met you. You can now put on your coat and go." As Welsh still sat defiantly, he added, "*At once,* sir! Or you may possibly find policemen and four-wheeled cabs outside. I have something else to say to Dr. Twiddel."

With the best air he could muster, Welsh silently cocked his hat on the side of his head, threw his coat over his arm, and was walking out, when a watchful waiter intercepted him.

"Your bill, sare."

"My friend is paying."

"No, Mr. Welsh," cried the real Essington; "I think you had better pay for this dinner yourself."

Welsh saw the vigilant proprietor already coming towards him, and with a look that augured ill for Twiddel when they were alone, he put his hand in his pocket.

"Ha, ha!" laughed Essington, "the inevitable bill!"

"And now," he continued, turning to Twiddel, "you, doctor, seem to me a most unfortunately constructed biped; your nose is just long enough to enable you to be led into a singularly original adventure, and your brains just too few to carry it through creditably. Hang me if I wouldn't have made a better job of the business! But before you disappear from the company of gentlemen I must ask you to do one favour for me. First thing tomorrow morning you will go down to Clankwood, tell what lie you please, and obtain my legal discharge, or whatever it's called. After that you may go to the devil—or, what comes much to the same thing, to Mr. Welsh—for all I care. You will do this without fail?"

"Ye—es," stammered Twiddel, "certainly, sir."

"You may now retire—and the faster the better."

As the crestfallen doctor followed his ally out of the restaurant, the Baron exclaimed in disgust, "Ze cads! You are too merciful. You should punish."

"My dear Baron, after all I am obliged to these rascals for the most amusing time I have ever had in my life, and one of the best friends I've ever made."

"Ach, Bonker! Bot vat do I say? You are not Bonker no more, and yet may I call you so, jost for ze sake of pleasant times? It vill be too hard to change."

"I'd rather you would, Baron. It will be a perpetual in memoriam record of my departed virtues."

"Departed, Bonker?"

"Departed, Baron," his friend repeated with a sigh; "for how can I ever hope to have so spacious a field for them again? Believe me, they will wither in an atmosphere of orthodoxy. And now let us order dinner."

"But first," said the Baron, blushing, "I haf a piece of news."

"Baron, I guess it!"

"Ze Lady Alicia is now mine! Congratulate!"

"With all my heart, Baron! What could be a fitter finish than the detection of villainy, the marriage of all the sane people, and the apotheosis of the lunatic?"

THE END.

—ALSO AVAILABLE FROM THE COLLINS LIBRARY—

English As She Is Spoke
by José da Fonseca and Pedro Carolino

Perhaps the worst foreign phrasebook ever written, this linguistic train wreck was first published in 1855 and became a classic of unintentional humor. In the preface to an American edition, Mark Twain wrote "Nobody can add to the absurdity of this book, nobody can imitate it successfully, nobody can hope to produce its fellow; it is perfect."

"This book has made me laugh so hard it almost hurts... Should be experienced by anyone who loves our language."

—*Washington Post*

The Riddle of the Traveling Skull
by Harry Stephen Keeler

In dozens of dumbfounding novels, Harry Stephen Keeler ecstatically catapulted the mystery genre into an absurdity that has yet to be equaled. This one begins with a cutting-edge handbag and grows to engulf experimental brain surgery, Legga the Human Spider, and the unlikely asylum state of San Do Mar. Things get stranger from there.

"You cannot possibly dream of anything half so bizarre as the yarn that Mr. Keeler has strung together." —*New York Times*

"Sometimes we wonder if anyone writing today is so vividly imaginative. We will say that Mr. Keeler is incomparable."

—*San Francisco Chronicle*

—ODDITIES THAT SHOULD NOT BE FORGOTTEN—